# BURNING PATIENCE

D0776041

A Pantheon Modern Writers Original

Translated from the Spanish
by Katherine Silver

**PANTHEON BOOKS NEW YORK**

# BURNING

Antonio    Skármeta

# PATIENCE

Translation Copyright © 1987 by Katherine Silver

All rights reserved under International and Pan-American Copyright Conventions. Published in the United States by Pantheon Books, a division of Random House, Inc., New York, and simultaneously in Canada by Random House of Canada Limited, Toronto.

Originally published in the United States in Spanish as *Ardiente Paciencia* by Ediciones del Norte, Hanover, N.H. Copyright © 1985 by Antonio Skármeta. Copyright © 1985 by Ediciones del Norte.

Library of Congress Cataloging-in-Publication Data
Skármeta, Antonio.
Burning patience.
1. Neruda, Pablo, 1904–1973, in fiction, drama,
poetry, etc.  I. Title.
PQ8098.29.K3A7313  1987      863      86-25285
ISBN 0-394-55576-7
ISBN 0-394-75033-0 (pbk.)

*Book design by Guenet Abraham*

Manufactured in the United States of America

First English Language Edition

To Matilde Urrutia, Neruda's inspiration,
and through him, that of his humble plagiarists.

# BURNING PATIENCE

**A**s a result of two trivial yet fortunate circumstances, Mario Jiménez launched himself on a new career in the month of June 1969. The first was his aversion to fishing—or, more to the point, an aversion to those tasks that required him to be out of bed before dawn, a propitious time of day for dreaming about daring affairs with women as passionate as those who appeared on the screen at the San Antonio Movie Theater. This habit, as well as a permanent susceptibility to real or invented colds, excused him, more often than not, from preparing the tackle for his father's boat, gave him full license to stay snuggling under thick ponchos from the southern islands, and allowed him to perfect his oneiric idylls until his father, José Jiménez, returned from the high seas, soaked and hungry, at which time Mario, to appease his own guilty conscience, prepared lunch: toasty fresh bread, a lively salad of tomatoes and onions with parsley and cilantro, and for himself an aspirin, which he dramatically ingested at the moment his progenitor's sarcasm penetrated the very marrow of his bones.

"Go get a job" was his father's brutal, straightforward statement, summing up an accusatory stare that had lasted at least five, if not ten, minutes.

"Sure, Dad," Mario answered, wiping his nose on the sleeve of his jacket.

The second circumstance consisted of Mario's possession of a cheery Legnano bicycle, which carried him beyond the rather limited horizon of the fishermen's bay and into the port of San Antonio which, though insignificant, seemed Babylonian in comparison to Mario's own little hamlet. The mere sight of those movie posters of women with promiscuous mouths, and tough guys with impeccable teeth chewing on cigars, sent him into a trance only two hours in a dark theater could possibly cure. Then he would bike dejectedly home, sometimes under a coastal drizzle that would make him even more vulnerable to viral infections of epic proportions. And since his father's generosity never fully met his voluptuous needs, he was often obliged to make do with a visit to a used-magazine stand where he could do nothing more than contribute to the wear and tear of the photographs of his favorite actresses.

It was on one such day that Mario happened to glimpse an ad in the window of the post office, and though it was written on a sheet of paper carelessly torn from a school mathematics notebook—a subject in which Mario had not excelled in grammar school—he could not resist.

He had never worn a tie in his life, but he straightened out his shirt collar as if he were wearing one and made a quick and only partially successful attempt to organize the locks he had cultivated in faithful imitation of the Beatles.

With a smile like Burt Lancaster's he announced to the functionary, "I've come in response to the ad."

"Do you own a bicycle?" the functionary asked indifferently.

"Yes," answered heart and lips in unison.

"Good," said the man as he wiped off his glasses. "We need a postman for Isla Negra."

"What a coincidence, I live right near there, at the bay."

"That's just fine. The bad part is that you'll have only one client."

"Only one?"

"That's right. Everybody else in the area is illiterate. They can't even read their bills."

"So who's the client?"

"Pablo Neruda."

Mario Jiménez swallowed what seemed like a quart of saliva. "But that's fantastic!"

"You think it's fantastic? He receives tons of mail every day. Riding your bicycle with that bag on your back is like carrying an elephant on your shoulders. The man who worked the route before you was hunched over like a camel when he retired."

"But I'm only seventeen."

"Are you in good health?"

"Me? In good health? I'm as strong as a horse. Never even had a runny nose."

The functionary slid his glasses down the bridge of his nose and peered at him over the top of the frame. "The salary isn't worth shit. The other postmen make it on their tips. But with just one client you'll only make enough to go to the movies once a week."

"I want the job."

"Okay. The name is Cosme."

"Cosme."

"You should call me *Mr.* Cosme."

"Of course, Mr. Cosme."

"I'm your boss."

"Okay, boss."

The man picked up his blue ball-point pen, blew on the tip to warm it up, and without looking asked, "Name?"

"Mario Jiménez," Mario Jiménez answered solemnly.

As soon as he had transmitted this vital piece of information, he walked over to the window, tore down the ad, and stuffed it into his back pocket.

..................................................................................

The sweet and simple San Antonio Post Office managed to effect a change that the Pacific Ocean, with its seemingly eternal patience, had never brought about: Mario Jiménez not only woke up whistling and with clear sinuses at the crack of dawn each day, but he fulfilled the duties of his profession so punctually that old Cosme entrusted him with a key to the office so that, one day, he could live out his own long-dreamt-of fantasy: to sleep until it was time to take a nap, to take such a long nap that it would be time to go to bed for the night, and to sleep so deeply all night that he would wake up the next morning overflowing with as much enthusiasm for work as Mario exuded on a daily basis and of which Cosme had never so much as had a taste.

When his first paycheck arrived—a month and a half late as is usual in Chile—Mario Jiménez, the postman, purchased the following items: one bottle of Special Vintage Cousiño Macul wine for his father; one ticket to see *West Side Story* starring Natalie Wood; a steel comb Made in Germany from a street vendor in the San Antonio market who had caught his attention with the sales pitch, "Germany lost the war but won the peace—stainless-steel combs made by Solingen"; and the Losada edition of *Elemental Odes* by his client and neighbor, Pablo Neruda.

He had made up his mind that, at an opportune moment, when the bard seemed to be in a good mood, he would hand the book over to him along with his mail in the hope of procuring an autograph he could subsequently boast about to hypothetical gorgeous women he would someday meet in San Antonio, or possibly even in Santiago, which he planned to visit upon receipt of his second check. Though on the verge of carrying out his plan a number of times, he was invariably stopped short by the sluggishness with which the poet received his mail, the promptness with which he handed him his tip (sometimes bigger than others), and the expression on his face of a man abysmally focused on his inner self. As it was, for months Mario was unable to shake the feeling that each time he rang the doorbell he was destroying the poet's inspiration just as he was about to embark on the composition of a brilliant new verse. Neruda always took the bundle of mail, gave him his few cents, and said good-bye with a smile as cursory as his glance. From that moment until the end of each day, the postman would carry around his copy of *Elemental Odes* in the hope of someday summoning up the necessary courage. He handled the book so much, and held it on his lap for so long under the light in the main square to impress the girls (who never even noticed his existence) with the fact that he was an intellectual, that in the end he actually read it. Once he had this accomplishment under his belt he felt he deserved a crumb of the bard's attention, and one morning of wintry sunshine he slipped the book on top of the pile of letters and accompanied it with a phrase he had practiced in front of many shop windows:

"Put it right there, maestro."

Fulfilling Mario's request was a routine task for the poet, and once it was completed he said good-bye with his characteristic curtness. Mario began to analyze the autograph and arrived at the conclusion that his own anonymity had not been seriously altered by the "Sincerely, Pablo Neruda." He now set himself the goal of striking up the kind of relationship with the poet that would one day merit his request for a dedication including, at least, his full name written in green ink: Mario Jiménez. Optimally, he imagined that the text would read something like: "To my intimate friend, Mario Jiménez. Pablo Neruda." He expressed these longings to Cosme, the telegraph operator, who reminded him that the Chilean Postal Service strictly prohibited its postmen from disturbing their clients with unusual requests and then informed him that one book could not be dedicated twice. In other words, by no means would it be advisable to ask the poet—even though he was a communist—to scratch out the words he had written and replace them with others.

Mario considered this to be sound advice, and when he received his second paycheck, he made what he thought was a logical purchase: the Losada edition of the *New Elemental Odes*. He felt a pang of regret at having given up his long-desired excursion to Santiago along with a quiver of excitement when the clever bookseller said, "And I'll have the *Third Book of Odes* for you by next month."

Neither of these books, however, was destined to be autographed by the poet. On another morning of pale, wintry sunshine, much like the one just mentioned, he forgot all about dedications but not, God forbid, about poetry.

...........................................................................................................

Young Mario Jiménez had been raised among fishermen, but he never so much as suspected that a hook for catching the poet would be contained in the morning mail. He had just handed the day's mail over to his client when one letter was plucked from the pile and torn open right there in the boy's presence. This unprecedented behavior, so out of keeping with the bard's usual serenity and discretion, kindled the postman's dying flames of hope for a dialogue and—why not admit it—maybe even a friendship.

"Why did you open that letter before the others?"

"Because it's from Sweden."

"And what's so special about Sweden besides Swedish women?"

At this, Pablo Neruda blinked his usually immutable eyelids.

"The Nobel Prize for Literature, my son."

"Are they going to give it to you?"

"If they do, I won't turn it down."

"How much is it for?"

The poet, who by now had gotten to the most important part of the letter, said casually, "One hundred and fifty thousand, two hundred and fifty dollars."

Mario could not help chuckling when he thought of adding, "and fifty cents," but his persistent impertinence was checked by a better instinct, and instead, in the coolest voice he could muster, he said, "Well?"

"Well, what?"

"Are they going to give it to you?"

"Perhaps. But this year there are others who seem to have better chances."

"How come?"

"Because they've written great works."

"And what about the rest of the letters?"

"I'll read them later," the bard sighed.

"Oh."

Mario, who had a sneaking suspicion that the dialogue was about to come to an end, took the liberty of drifting into a state of absentmindedness similar to that common in his only and favorite client. Mario's lapse was so total, however, that the poet felt compelled to ask, "What are you thinking about?"

"Oh, just about what might be in your other letters. Maybe they're love letters?"

The robust bard coughed. "Listen, I'm a married man. I hope Matilde didn't hear you."

"I'm sorry, sir."

Neruda dug into his pocket and brought out a bill of a "higher than usual" denomination. The postman said thank you in a tone of distress undoubtedly due to the imminent parting and not to the size of the tip. Whatever its source, his distress was quickly transformed into an alarming degree of paralysis. The poet, who was preparing to turn back to his house, could not help but wonder at such extreme inertia.

"What's the matter with you?"

"Sir?"

"You're standing there like a post."

Mario twisted his head around and met the poet's eyes. "Riveted like a nail."

"No. As still as a rook."

"Calmer than a porcelain cat?"

Neruda released the latch on the gate and rubbed his chin. "Mario Jiménez, I have books that are much better than *Elemental Odes*. It is shameful of you to subject me to all those comparisons and metaphors."

"Sir?"

"Metaphors, I said!"

"What's that?"

The poet placed his hand on the boy's shoulder.

"To be more or less imprecise, we could say that it is a way of describing something by comparing it to something else."

"Give me an example."

Neruda looked at his watch and sighed.

"Well, when you say the sky is weeping, what do you mean?"

"That's easy—that it's raining."

"So, you see, that's a metaphor."

"But, if it's such a simple thing, why does it have such a complicated name?"

"Because the names of things have nothing whatsoever to do with how simple or complicated they are.

According to you, a small thing that flies around should not have a name as long as *butterfly*. *Elephant*, after all, has fewer letters than *butterfly*," he concluded, by now quite out of breath, "and it is much bigger and doesn't fly." Then, with all of his remaining energy, he indicated to Mario that he should now be on his way towards the bay.

The postman maintained his presence of mind and added, "Wow! I sure would like to be a poet!"

"You know what? Everybody and his brother is a poet in Chile. Being a postman is much more original. At least you get to walk a lot and you don't get fat. In Chile, all of us poets have big potbellies."

Neruda again took hold of the latch and was ready to enter when Mario, watching the flight of an invisible bird, said. "It's just that if I were a poet, I could say whatever I wanted to."

"What do you want to say?"

"Well, that's just the problem. Since I'm not a poet, I can't say it."

The bard knitted his brow.

"Mario—"

"Yes, sir?"

"I'm going to say good-bye now and close the gate."

"Okay, sir."

"See you tomorrow."

"Yeah, see you tomorrow."

Neruda rested his eyes on the remaining letters, then peeked out through the gate. The postman was standing there with his arms folded over his chest, studying the clouds. The poet went up to him and poked him on the shoulder.

"I've returned because I suspected you were still out here."

"I just got to thinking."

Neruda tightened his grip around the postman's elbow and led him firmly to the lamppost where his bicycle was parked.

"And you think you can think just standing there? If you want to be a poet, you have to be able to think while you walk. Or are you like John Wayne, who can't walk and chew gum at the same time? You are now going to walk along the beach to the bay and as you observe the movement of the sea, you are going to invent metaphors."

"Give me an example!"

"Listen to this poem: 'Here on the Island, the sea, so much sea. It spills over from time to time. It says yes, then no, then no. It says yes, in blue, in foam, in a gallop. It says no, then no. It cannot be still. My name is sea, it repeats, striking a stone but not convincing it. Then with the seven green tongues, of seven green tigers, of seven green seas, it caresses it, kisses it, wets it, and pounds on its chest, repeating its own name.' "

He paused with an air of satisfaction. "What do you think?"

"It's weird."

"Weird? You certainly are a severe critic."

"No, sir. The *poem* wasn't weird. What was weird was the way *I* felt when you recited it."

"My dear Mario, please try to express yourself more clearly. I simply cannot spend the whole morning in your delightful company."

"How can I explain it to you? When you recited that poem, the words went from over there to over here."

"Like the sea, then!"

"Yeah, they moved just like the sea."

"That's the rhythm."

"And I felt weird because with all that movement, I got dizzy."

"You got dizzy?"

"Of course. I was like a boat tossing upon your words."

The poet's eyelids rose slowly.

"Like a boat tossing upon my words."

"Uh-huh."

"You know what you just did, Mario?"

"No, what?"

"You invented a metaphor."

"But it doesn't count, 'cause it just came out by accident."

"All images are accidents, my son."

Mario placed his hand over his heart in an attempt to control the wild palpitations. He was sure his chest would burst open right there. But he pulled himself together, and with one impertinent finger shaking just inches away from his emeritus client's nose, said, "Do you think that everything in the world, I mean *everything*, like the wind, the ocean, trees, mountains, fire, animals, houses, deserts, the rain . . ."

"Now you can say 'etcetera.' "

". . . all the etceteras. Do you think the whole world is a metaphor for something?"

Neruda's mouth gaped and his robust chin seemed ready to drop right off his face.

"Did I ask a stupid question?"

"No, my friend, no."

"It's just that you got such a weird expression on your face."

"No. I just got to thinking."

With a sweep of his hand, he brushed an imaginary mist from his eyes, hitched up his drooping pants, and sticking his index finger into the young man's chest said, "Look, Mario, let's make a deal. I am now going to go into my kitchen, prepare myself an aspirin sandwich, and meditate on your question. Tomorrow I will give you my considered opinion."

"Really, sir?"

"Yes, really. Now, good-bye. I'll see you tomorrow."

He turned back towards the house and, after closing the gate, leaned against it and patiently folded his arms.

"Aren't you going inside?" Mario asked.

"Oh no. This time I'm going to wait until you leave."

The postman picked up his bicycle, joyously rang its bell, and with a smile wide enough to encompass the poet and his immediate surroundings, shouted, "See you later, sir."

"See you later, son."

Mario Jiménez, the postman, took the poet's words literally, and carefully scrutinized the ocean's comings and goings as he walked along the coast towards his village. But in spite of an abundance of waves, an immaculate afternoon, luxurious sand, and a fresh breeze, he could not produce even one single metaphor. The sea's vast eloquence resounded only with silence, for Mario was so stubbornly aphonic that even the rocks seemed gregarious by comparison.

Fed up with the sullenness of nature, he talked himself into visiting the tavern to drown his sorrows in wine, and, if fortune shone upon him, challenge a fellow loafer to a game of taca-taca. (Without a football stadium in the village, the local youth had to satisfy their athletic yearnings at this little table of mini-soccer.)

While still at some distance, Mario heard the clanging of the metallic balls accompanying the scratchy sounds of the old Wurlitzer playing "Mucho Amor" by the Ramblers, a song still popular in the village despite its eclipse in the capital more than a decade earlier. Feeling the urgent need to stave off his depression, he entered the tavern with the idea of converting the poet's tip into wine, but before he could do so, he was overwhelmed by an intoxication that spirits had never in his brief life afforded him.

There at the table, playing with the rusty blue knobs, sat the most beautiful girl he had ever seen, actresses, usherettes, hairdressers, schoolgirls, tourists, and record store clerks notwithstanding. Although his desire for girls was equalled only by his timidity—a situation that had often left him floundering in frustration—he approached the taca-taca table with the daring of a sleep-walker. As he stood behind the red side's goal, he tried to hide his fascination by focusing his beady eyes upon the ball's movements, but this was completely ineffectual. When the girl registered a goal on the metal score-keeper, he looked straight at her and flashed her the most seductive smile he could muster. She responded to this courtesy by advising him to take charge of the rival team's front line. Until that moment, Mario had barely noticed that the girl had been playing with a friend and he only learned of the other's existence after he slammed into her and sent her flying towards the defense. Few times in his life had he been so aware of the beating of his heart. The blood pounded through his veins so violently that he had to rest his hand on his chest in an attempt to calm the flow. The girl hit the white ball against the side and pretended to guide it into the other team's goal, and just as Mario was about to maneuver his players to impress her with the dexterity of his wrists, the girl picked up the ball and placed it in between her teeth, where it shone for all it was worth. She then pushed out her chest—covered by a blouse at least two sizes too small for those persuasive breasts—and offered him the ball to pluck from her mouth. Both humiliated and hypnotized, the postman lifted his trem-bling right hand, and just as his fingers were about to touch the ball, the girl moved away, leaving him with nothing but a mocking smile. There he stood, his arm suspended in midair, as if he were proposing a ridiculous toast without either a glass or champagne to a love that would never be consummated. Swinging her body and legs to a rhythm much more evocative than that of the Ramblers, she slunk over to the bar. Mario had no need for a mirror to know that his face was red and sweaty. The other girl slipped into the vacated spot and hit the ball sharply in an attempt to awaken Mario from his trance. The postman looked up dejectedly into his new rival's eyes, and in spite of having declared to the Pacific Ocean that he was inept at comparisons and metaphors, told himself defiantly that to play with this plain villager would be *a)* less exciting than dancing with his own sister, *b)* more boring than a Sunday afternoon without football, and *c)* about as thrilling as a snail race.

Without so much as a parting nod, he followed his beloved's footsteps right up to the bar, collapsed into a chair as if it were a seat in a theater, and for long moments watched in ecstasy as the girl blew into heavy wineglasses and rubbed them with a cloth embroidered with lily plants until they were spotless and shiny.

.....................................................................................

Cosme, the telegraph operator, held two principles dear. One was socialism, about which he harangued his subordinates despite the fact that they were all either sympathizers or activists already. The second was the wearing of the post office cap inside the office. He managed to tolerate Mario's tangled mop of hair that surpassed the Beatles' in proletarian spirit alone, his blue jeans infested with oil stains from the chain of his bicycle, his faded workman's jacket, and that habit he had of exploring his nose with his little finger. But his blood came to a boil at the sight of Mario bareheaded. So when the emaciated postman came in and started over to the sorting table after saying an anemic "Good morning," Cosme stopped him in his tracks, placed a stiff finger on his neck, led him over to the hat rack, pulled a cap down over his ears, and only then allowed him to safely repeat his greeting.

"Good morning, boss."

"Good morning," Cosme grumbled.

"Any letters for the poet?"

"Yeah, lots. And there's a telegram too."

"A telegram!"

The boy grabbed it, held it up to the light in an attempt to read its contents, and in a shot was out the door and mounting his bicycle. He was already pedaling away as Cosme shouted from the doorway:

"You forgot the rest of the letters."

"I'll come back for them," he yelled as he pedaled away.

"You're a fool," Cosme shouted again. "You'll have to make two trips."

"I'm no fool, boss. This way I get to see the poet twice."

At Neruda's gate, he rang the bell longer than any conceivable rule of etiquette would sanction. Three minutes of such behavior, however, failed to make the poet appear, so he leaned his bicycle against the lamp-post and, with a burst of energy, ran down to the rocks along the beach, where he found Neruda on his hands and knees digging in the sand.

"I got lucky," he shouted as he approached, leaping over the boulders. "Telegram!"

"You must have gotten up at the crack of dawn, my boy."

When Mario reached his side, he dedicated ten seconds of panting and heaving to the poet while catching his breath.

"I don't care. I'm lucky because I have to have a talk with you."

"It must be important. You're snorting like a horse."

Mario wiped the sweat off his forehead with a sweep of his hand, dried the telegram on his legs, and placed it in the poet's hand.

"Don Pablo," he declared solemnly, "I'm in love."

The bard held the telegram like a fan and waved it in front of his chin.

"Now, now," he responded. "It's not all that serious. There are remedies."

"Remedies? Don Pablo, if there's a remedy for this, I only want to be sick. I'm in love, head over heels in love."

The next two words the poet uttered seemed to fall like separate stones from his mouth.

"Against whom?"

"Don Pablo?"

"With whom, my son?"

"Her name is Beatriz."

"Damn! Dante!"

"Don Pablo?"

"There was once a poet named Dante who fell in love with a woman named Beatriz. It seems that Beatrizes provoke incommensurable loves."

The postman whipped his Bic pen out of his pocket and began to write on the palm of his left hand.

"What are you doing?"

"I'm writing down that poet's name—Dante?"

"Dante Alighieri."

"Is that spelled with an *H*?"

"No, my son, with an *A*."

"*A* as in animal?"

"As in animal and instinct."

"Don Pablo?"

The poet took out his own green pen, placed the boy's hand on the rock, and wrote out the name in grandiose letters. Just as the poet was about to open the telegram, Mario slapped his own forehead with his now illustrious palm and sighed.

"Don Pablo, I'm in love."

"You already said that. But how can *I* be of service to you?"

"You can help me."

"At my age?"

"You have to help me because I don't know what to say to her. When I see her right there in front of me I go dumb. I can't utter a single word."

"What? You mean you haven't spoken to her?"

"Hardly anything. Yesterday I walked along the beach just like you told me to. I watched the sea for a long time but I couldn't think of one single metaphor. Then I went to the tavern and bought a bottle of wine. Anyway, she's the one who sold it to me."

"Beatriz."

"Beatriz. I stayed there staring at her and fell in love."

"So quickly?"

"No, not *so* quickly. I stared at her for about ten minutes."

"And what did she do?"

"She said, 'What are you looking at? Is there something wrong with my face or something?' "

"And you?"

"I couldn't think of anything to say."

"Nothing? You didn't utter a word?"

"Well, it's not as bad as all that. I said five words."

"Which ones?"

" 'What's your name?' "

"And she?"

"She said 'Beatriz González.' "

"You asked her 'What's your name?' That's only three words. What were the other two?"

"Beatriz González."

"Beatriz González?"

"She said 'Beatriz González' and I repeated 'Beatriz González.' "

"Listen, my boy, you have brought me an urgent telegram and if we keep talking about Beatriz González the message is going to rot in my hands."

"Okay, open it up."

"As a postman you should know that one's correspondence is private."

"I've never opened any of your letters."

"I didn't say that you have. What I meant to say is that everyone has the right to read his own letters calmly, without the presence of spies or witnesses."

"I understand, Don Pablo."

"I'm glad."

Mario, overwhelmed with anguish and sweat, whispered in a sullen voice, "See you later, poet."

"See you later, Mario."

Hoping to put an end to this episode with a touch of generosity, the bard handed him a bill of the "very good" category. But Mario only contemplated it with additional anguish and said as he handed it back, "If it wouldn't be too much bother, I'd rather have you write me a poem for her instead of giving me the money."

Neruda had not run in years, but he now felt such a compulsion to remove himself from this landscape along with the migratory birds Bécquer had sung about so sweetly, that he took off down the beach as speedily as possible, given his age and physical condition, lifting his arms into the air in a gesture of utter hopelessness. "But I don't even know her! A poet needs to know someone to be inspired. I can't just invent something out of nothing."

"Look," the postman said as he followed him. "If you make such a big fuss out of a simple poem, you'll never get the Nobel Prize."

Neruda stopped, out of breath.

"Mario, please, I beg you to pinch me and wake me from this nightmare."

"So what do I tell her, Don Pablo? You are the only person in the whole town who can help me. All the others are fishermen who don't know how to say anything."

"But those fishermen also fell in love and managed to say something to the girls they liked."

"Fish stories!"

"But they courted them and married them. What does your father do?"

"He's a fisherman."

"There you are! At one time he must have talked to your mother and persuaded her to marry him."

"Don Pablo, that's not a fair comparison because Beatriz is much more beautiful than my mother."

"My dear Mario, I can no longer resist the temptation to read this telegram. Will you please be so kind as to allow me to do so?"

"With pleasure."

"Thank you."

Neruda wanted only to tear open the envelope, but in his hurry he ripped apart the entire telegram. Standing on the tips of his toes, Mario tried to get a glimpse over the poet's shoulder.

"It's not from Sweden, is it?"

"No."

"Do you think they'll give you the Nobel Prize this year?"

"I'm not particularly worried about that any more. I get sick of seeing my name in the yearly competition as if I were a race horse."

"Who's the telegram from, then?"

"The Central Committee of the Party."

The poet paused with a tragic air.

"Son, is today Friday the thirteenth by any chance?"

"Bad news?"

"Terrible! They've chosen me as candidate for president of the Republic of Chile!"

"But Don Pablo, that's wonderful!"

"It's wonderful to be chosen, but what if I get elected?"

"Of course you will. Everyone knows you. My father has only one book in his house and it's yours."

"What does that prove?"

"What do you mean, what does that prove? The fact that my father doesn't know how to read or write and has one of your books means that we'll win."

"*We'll* win?"

"Of course. I'll vote for you no matter what."

"Thank you for your support."

Neruda folded the telegram's mortal remains and buried them in his back pocket. The postman was staring at him with such a mournful look in his eyes that he reminded the bard of a puppy standing in the mist in his hometown of Parral.

Without even smiling, he said, "Now let's go to the tavern and meet your famous Beatriz González."

"Don Pablo, you're joking?"

"No, I'm serious. Let's go to the bar, have a sip of wine, and take a look at your girlfriend."

"She's going to die when she sees us together. Pablo Neruda and Mario Jiménez drinking wine in the tavern! She'll die!"

"That would be very sad. Then you would have to write her an epitaph instead of a poem." The bard began walking energetically, but when he saw that Mario was lagging behind, he turned around and said, "What's the matter now?"

The postman ran up alongside him and looked him in the eye. "Don Pablo, if I get married to Beatriz González, will you be the godfather of the wedding?"

Neruda rubbed his perfectly shaved chin, pretended to weigh the question, and then rested his finger apodictically upon his forehead.

"After drinking some wine at the tavern, we are going to come to decisions on both of these issues."

"Both of *what* issues?"

"The presidency and Beatriz González."

..............................................................................................

When the lone fisherman at the tavern saw Pablo Neruda approaching with an anonymous youth who appeared to be tied to a leather bag, he alerted the new innkeeper to the arrival of an at least partially distinguished clientele.

"You've got customers."

The newcomers sat down where they could observe a girl approximately seventeen years old as she crossed behind the bar on her way towards their table. She had curly, wind-tossed brown hair, melancholic yet self-confident brown eyes as round as ripe cherries, a neckline that swept into breasts sadistically oppressed by that white blouse two sizes too small, nipples that took their stand even when covered, and one of those waists fit to grab to dance the tango with until the break of dawn or the last drop of wine has been drunk. In a moment her customers were able to appreciate her body in its full-length splendor as she stepped onto the dining room floor. Her waist spread out into a pair of hips whose dizzying effect was further exaggerated by a miniskirt that carried the eye down her legs, past her copper-colored knees and right into a pair of plump, rustic bare feet. A renewed and more thorough voyage up through each of her attributes ended at those brown eyes that had changed their expression from sadness to malice as soon as she recognized her guests.

"So, look who's here, the king of taca-taca," Beatriz González said as her little finger pressed against the oilskin tablecloth. "What can I get for you?"

Mario fixed his eyes on hers and for half a minute tried to convince his brain to supply him with the minimum information necessary to overcome this crisis he was experiencing: Who am I, where am I, how do you breathe, how do you talk?

Even after the girl had repeated her question and

drummed a whole handful of fragile fingers on the table, Mario could only maintain his perfect silence. Beatriz González then turned inquisitively towards his companion and, with a modulated voice and a flash of her tongue, asked a question Neruda would have considered routine under almost any other circumstance.

"And for you?"

"The same as him," the bard announced.

Two days later a boisterous truck plastered with posters of the bard and "Neruda for President" slogans arrived in town and kidnapped him from his retreat. The poet summarized his impressions in his journal: "Political life fell upon me like a thunderbolt and separated me from my work. The masses of humanity have been the greatest teacher I have had. I can approach them with the innate timidity of a poet or the caution of a shy man, but once among them, I feel transformed. I am part of the essential majority; I am but one more leaf on the great human tree."

Mario Jiménez, a rather wilted leaf of this very same tree, came to say good-bye. He was not even remotely consoled when the poet, after embracing him rather ceremoniously, presented him with two leather-bound volumes of his complete works, replete with a dedication—"To my dear friend and comrade, Mario Jiménez. Pablo Neruda"—that otherwise would have surpassed his highest hopes.

He watched the truck disappear down the dirt road and wished that the dust rising in its wake would bury him as if he were already dead.

Out of strict loyalty to the poet, he swore not to commit suicide until he had read every single one of the three thousand pages he had been given. He did his duty to the first fifty as he sat at the foot of the bell tower; but the very same sea that inspired the poet with so many resplendent images only distracted Mario with its chantlike repetition of "Beatriz González, Beatriz González."

His next few days were spent hanging around the tavern, the two volumes of poems strapped to his bicycle rack, and a school notebook that he had purchased in San Antonio to fill with images inspired by the torrential lyrics of the master, firmly in his grip. The fishermen observed him toiling away with pencil in hand, languidly staring off to sea, but they had no idea that he was only filling the pages with carelessly drawn circles and triangles as meaningless as the boy's own thoughts. It took but a few hours for word to spread through the entire village that with Pablo Neruda out of the way, Mario Jiménez, his postman, was attempting to usurp his kingdom. Obsessively occupied with every last minuscule detail of his misery, Mario was oblivious to these rumors until, one afternoon while sitting on a breakwater where the fishermen sold their catch, reading through the last pages of *Extravagario*, he suddenly heard a truck with loudspeakers broadcasting the slogan, "Halt the spread of Marxism with Chile's best candidate, Jorge Alessandri"; and another, if not as ingenious at least more veracious, "Jorge Alessandri Rodríguez, a man with experience in government." The truck stopped. Two men dressed in white alighted and walked over to the fishermen while flashing plethoric smiles, a rare sight in that part of the world where a paucity of teeth forestalled such excesses. One of the men was Labbé, the right-wing deputy of the region, who had won the last election on the promise of bringing electricity to the village. The closest he had ever come to fulfilling his pledge was to install a stop light at the intersection of two dirt roads where the only traffic was the truck that came to collect the fish, Mario's Legnano bicycle, donkeys, dogs, and bewildered chickens.

"Well, here we are, working for Alessandri," he said as he passed out leaflets.

With a cordiality well-learned through years of left-wing politics and illiteracy, the fishermen accepted them, looked at the picture of the ancient ex-president—his facial expression perfectly mirroring his austere preachings and practices—and stuffed them into their shirt-pockets. Only Mario handed his back.

"I'm going to vote for Neruda," he said.

The deputy's generous smile, first intended only for Mario, now took in the whole group of fishermen. Everyone was immediately won over by his charming manner, an effect Alessandri undoubtedly counted on when he chose this man to campaign among fishermen, so well-versed in hooking fish and avoiding being hooked themselves.

"Neruda," Labbé repeated, forcing the syllables of the bard's name along each one of his pearly teeth, "Neruda is a great poet. Perhaps the greatest of all poets. But frankly, gentlemen, I cannot imagine him as president of Chile."

He offered the leaflet to Mario again and said, "Just read it, my boy. Maybe it will change your mind."

The postman placed the folded sheet in his pocket while the deputy bent down to look at some clams in a basket.

"How much a dozen?"

"For you, sir, only one hundred and fifty."

"One hundred and fifty? At that price you'll have to guarantee I'll find a pearl in each one."

The fishermen all laughed along with Labbé, who, like many rich Chileans, had a way of infusing a sense of ease and comfort into the very air around him. He then stood up, walked a few steps away from Mario, and with a smile that had become almost beatific, said in a voice just loud enough for everyone to hear, "I understand you're getting interested in poetry. They say you're competing with Pablo Neruda."

The fishermen's laughter rose as quickly as the blush in Mario's cheeks. He felt suffocated, choked, embarrassed, confused, paralyzed, awkward, pink, scarlet, bright red, vermilion, purple, sweaty, defeated, trapped. When he could finally formulate a few words into a sentence, it was, "I want to die."

With a princely gesture, the deputy indicated to his assistant that he remove something from his leather briefcase. A moment later, a book with gilt lettering and bound in blue leather shone forth under the bay's sun. It was so fine, the bard's volumes appeared crude by comparison.

Labbé's eyes expressed deep affection as he handed Mario the book. "Here, my boy. This is for you."

Slowly, deliciously, the blush left Mario's face. It was as if a fresh wave had swept over him and then a breeze had come to dry him off and make life tolerable once again. He took a deep breath, flashed a smile more proletarian than Labbé's, though every bit as charming, ran his fingers along the polished surface of the blue leather, and said, "Thank you, Mr. Labbé."

.......................................................................................................

The pages of Mario's new book were so satiny, so immaculately white, that he felt quite justified in not soiling them with the likes of his own verses. Only after he had covered all the pages of his notebooks with doodles and disinfected his hands with Flores de Pravia soap would he pick out his very best metaphors and transcribe them onto those pages with a green pen just like the bard's own. During the following weeks, his fecundity grew in indirect proportion to his fame as a poet. His flirtation with the muses had been so well publicized that word had even reached the telegraph operator, who as a result recruited Mario to read a few of his poems at a political-cultural event of the Socialist Party of San Antonio. The postman agreed, but struck a compromise whereby he read Neruda's "Ode to the Wind." This won him a small ovation and the call for him to entertain militants and sympathizers alike at other such meetings with, for instance, a reading of Neruda's "Ode to Eel Stew." Right then and there, Cosme proposed and organized another evening for the cultural edification of the fishermen of the port.

But his public appearances and the indolence into which he had sunk without even one postal client did nothing to mitigate his longing for Beatriz González, who, though her beauty became more perfect by the day, was completely oblivious to the effect she was having on the poor postman.

Having memorized a considerable number of the bard's poems, Mario was about to embark on the first phase of a well-planned seduction when he came up against one of Chile's more terrifying institutions: the mother-in-law. One morning he stood under the lamppost on the corner near Beatriz's house and patiently pretended not to be waiting for her. When he saw her step through the door, he rushed forward uttering her name and found himself face to face with her mother, who looked at him as if he were an insect and said "Good morning" in a tone of voice that distinctly meant "Get lost."

The next day, opting for a more diplomatic strategy, he walked up to the bar of the tavern when he knew his beloved was not there, placed his bag on the counter, and asked her mother for a bottle of good wine. Slipping the bottle into his bag, he cleared his throat, looked around the dining room as if seeing it for the first time, and said, "Nice place you've got here."

Beatriz's mother responded courteously, "I didn't ask for your opinion."

Mario stared hard at his leather bag, and restraining the impulse to sink into the floorboards, cleared his throat again and said, "Neruda's mail's piling up. I carry it around so it won't get lost."

The woman crossed her arms over her chest and lifted her churlish nose. "So why tell me? You want to get me into a conversation or something?"

Encouraged by this fraternal communication, Mario followed Beatriz along the beach at dusk just as the orange sun was becoming the stuff of apprentice lovers and poets. When they reached the rocks—not realizing her mother was watching from the balcony of her house—he began to speak to her, his heart in his throat. First with vehemence and then as if he were a puppet and Neruda the ventriloquist, he gained such fluency that images flowed out of him magically and the conversation—or rather the recital—lasted until dark.

Afterwards, Beatriz walked directly back to the tavern, stunned some fishermen by absentmindedly lifting a half-consumed bottle of wine off their table as they hummed the bolero "La vela" by Roberto Lecaros, and headed for her house, loot in hand. Her mother suddenly decided closing time had come, excused her frustrated clients from having to pay their bill, and locked the place up.

She found her daughter in her room, her breast

exposed to the autumn wind and her gaze pursuing the oblique full moon that spread its diffuse light over the bed.

"What are you doing?" she asked.

"I'm thinking."

Without warning, her mother switched on the bright overhead light.

"If you're thinking, I want to see your face while you're thinking," her mother said as Beatriz turned her head, trying to shield her eyes from the light with her hands. "And with the window open in the middle of winter!"

"Mother, it's my room."

"Yeah, but I pay the doctor's bills. Let's not beat around the bush. Who is he?"

"His name is Mario."

"What does he do?"

"He's a postman."

"A postman?"

"What, haven't you seen his bag?"

"Of course I've seen it. I also saw that he uses it to carry around bottles of wine."

"He was already off work."

"Who does he deliver letters to?"

"To Don Pablo."

"Neruda?"

"They're friends."

"Did he tell you that?"

"I saw them together. They were sitting and talking in the tavern the other day."

"What were they talking about?"

"Politics."

"Oh no, so he's a communist too?!"

"Mother, Neruda is going to be the next president of Chile."

"My dear, if you start confusing poetry with politics, you'll end up a single mother. What did he say to you?"

Beatriz had the word on the tip of her tongue, where she held it for a few seconds to savor its connotations.

"Metaphors."

Her mother held onto the knob of the tarnished bronze bedstand and squeezed it as hard as she could.

"What's the matter, Mother? What's come over you?"

The woman fell onto the bed as if in a swoon and in a weary voice said, "I've just never heard you say such a long word. What 'metaphors' did he tell you?"

"He said . . . he said that my smile stretches across my face like a butterfly."

"What else?"

"Well, when he said that I laughed."

"Then what?"

"Then he said something about my laugh. He said my laugh was a rose, crashing water. He said my laugh was a sudden silvery wave."

The woman wet her shaking lips with her tongue.

"Then what did you do?"

"I kept quiet."

"What about him?"

"What else did he *say*?"

"No, my child. What else did he *do*? Because your postman must have hands as well as a mouth."

"He never touched me. He said he was happy to be next to a pure young woman, for it was like being on the shores of a white ocean."

"And you?"

"I just stood there thinking."

"And him?"

"He said he liked it when I was silent, for it was as if I were absent."

"And you?"

"I looked at him."

"And him?"

"He looked at me, too. Then he stopped looking me in the eyes and looked at my hair for a long time without saying anything, as if he were thinking. And then he said, 'I lack the time to celebrate your hair. I should describe and praise it, strand by strand.' "

Her mother stood up and crossed the palms of her hands over her chest as if they were guillotine blades.

"My dear, tell me no more. We are in the thick of a very dangerous situation. All men who first touch with words go much further afterwards with their hands."

"How could words be bad?" Beatriz said, hugging the pillow.

"There isn't a drug in the world worse than all that blah-blah-blah. It makes a village innkeeper feel like a Venetian princess. Later, when the moment of truth arrives, when life catches up with you, you'll realize that those words are no better than a bad check. I would much rather have a drunkard in the bar grab your ass than have someone tell you that your smile flies higher than a butterfly."

Beatriz jumped. "*Stretches* like a butterfly!"

"Flying or stretching doesn't make any difference! And you want to know why? Because there isn't anything behind those words. They're like fireworks that disintegrate in thin air."

"The words Mario said to me haven't disintegrated in thin air. I know them by heart and I like to think about them while I'm working."

"Yeah, I noticed. Tomorrow you pack your bags; you're going to stay with your aunt in Santiago for a few days."

"But I don't want to."

"I don't care what you want. This is getting way too serious."

"What's so serious about some guy talking to me? It happens to all the girls!"

Her mother tied a knot in her shawl.

"First of all, you can tell from a mile away that the things he says are copied right out of Neruda."

Beatriz twisted her neck around and looked up at the wall as if it were the horizon.

"No, Mother! He looked at me and the words fell right out of his mouth like birds."

"Out of his mouth like birds, huh? You're packing your bags and going tonight! You know what it's called when someone says something someone else has already said without saying who said it first? Plagiarism! Your

Mario could end up in jail for telling you . . . *metaphors*!
I will personally call the poet and tell him that his
postman is going around stealing his poems."

"How can you even imagine that Don Pablo would
care about that? He's a candidate for president of Chile
and they'll probably give him the Nobel Prize, and
you're going to go and make a fuss over a few metaphors."

The woman rubbed her thumb over her nose just
like a professional boxer.

"A few metaphors, huh? Just look at yourself!"

She grabbed the girl by her ear and pulled her
forward until their noses were touching.

"Mother!"

"You are as humid as a plant. You have the kind of
fever, my child, that can only be cured in two ways: a
good beating or a little trip." She let go of the girl's ear,
pulled a suitcase out from under the bed, and threw it
on the mattress. "Start packing!"

"No, I won't. I'm staying here!"

"My dear, rivers carry stones, and words, babies. The
suitcase!"

"I know how to take care of myself."

"What do you know about taking care of yourself? In
the state you're in right now, a breath of air would
knock you over. Just remember, I read Neruda a long
time before you did. I know full well that when men
reach their boiling point, they start getting poetic."

"Neruda is a serious person. He's going to be president."

"When you're talking about getting into the sack, there's not an ounce of difference between a president, a priest, or a communist poet. You know who wrote, 'I love the love of sailors who kiss and then are gone. They never leave a promise, never to return'?"

"Neruda!"

"Of course, Neruda. And you still think you're a smart cookie?"

"I wouldn't make such a big deal out of a little kiss."

"Out of a kiss, no. But a kiss is just the spark that starts the prairie fire. And here's another of Neruda's poems: 'I love the love dealt out in kisses, bed, and bread.' In other words, my child, and without beating around the bush, this thing even comes with breakfast in bed."

"Mother!"

"And then your postman is going to recite to you that immortal Neruda poem that I copied down in my journal when I was exactly your age, young lady: 'I do not want it, my love, nothing that binds us, nothing that unites us.'"

"I don't understand that one."

With her hands her mother traced the outline of an imaginary balloon that began at her belly button, reached its greatest volume over her lower abdomen, and tapered off at her hips. She accompanied these fluid movements with another recitation of the verse, this time with each of its syllables carefully enunciated: "I-do-not-want-it-my-love-no-thing-that-binds-us-no-thing-that-u-nites-us."

The perplexed girl watched the movements of her mother's hands and only then, inspired by the symbol of widowhood on her finger, asked in a birdlike voice, "The ring?"

After the death of her legitimate husband—Beatriz's father—the woman had sworn never to cry again until the day another member of her family should die. But now, at least one tear dropped off her eyelashes.

"Yes, my dear. The ring. Now, just pack your bags quietly."

The girl bit the pillow as if to prove that her mouth could rip apart fabric or meat as well as seduce, then shouted, "This is ridiculous. A man tells me that my smile flutters across my face like a butterfly and I have to go to Santiago."

"Don't be a fool!" her mother exploded. "*Now* your smile is like a butterfly, but tomorrow your tits are going to be two cooing doves, your nipples two juicy raspberries, your tongue the warm carpet of the gods, your behind the sails of a ship, and that thing burning there between your legs the furnace where the proud, erect metal of the race is forged. Now, good night!"

..............................................................................................

Mario walked around for days choking on his metaphors while Beatriz remained locked in her room, or, when out shopping or on a walk along the cliffs, with her mother's claws firmly dug into her forearm. He would

follow them from a short distance, hiding behind the
dunes along the way, knowing full well that his presence
was like a great stone tied around that woman's neck.
Every time the girl tried to turn her head, she was
brought up with a yank on her ear, a rather painful
gesture even if it was intended for her own good.

In the afternoons, he would stand outside the tavern
listening, inconsolable, to "La vela," always with the
undying hope that each passing shadow would bring in
its wake the miniskirt he now so often dreamt about
lifting ceremoniously with the tip of his tongue. In
keeping with his youthful mysticism, he was determined
not to alleviate his faithful and ever-present erection by
any manual manipulation. Instead, he hid it under the
bard's volumes during the day and sweated through
the tortures of temptation at night. He imagined, with
understandable romanticism, that each metaphor he
coined, every sigh he heaved, every image he conjured
up of her tongue between his legs or wetting his ear,
was just another contribution to a cosmic force strength-
ening his life juices. Then, on some distant day when
God decided to prove His existence by placing her in
his arms—either by giving her mother heart failure or
helping him in a desperate attempt to kidnap her—he
would levitate her right off the ground with gallons of
this improved substance.

On Sunday of the same week, the red truck that, only
two months before, had swept Neruda away brought
him back to Isla Negra. The vehicle was now plastered
with posters of a stern but tender and fatherly face

perched above a chest as noble as a dove's. Under each picture was written the name of Salvador Allende.

The fishermen began to run alongside the truck and Mario followed suit, vividly displaying his lack of athletic training. At the gate of his house, Neruda, wearing a poncho folded up over his shoulders and his classic cap, improvised a speech that, though brief, seemed to Mario to be eternal.

"My candidacy caught on like wildfire," the bard said as he deeply inhaled the aroma of the ocean. "They clamored for my presence wherever I went. I was deeply moved by those hundreds of humble men and women who held me, kissed me, and cried. I spoke to them all and I read them my poetry, sometimes in the pouring rain, sometimes on muddy streets and roads, sometimes in that bracing polar south wind that makes the very bones tremble. My enthusiasm was growing. More and more people attended my rallies. More and more women kept coming."

The fishermen laughed.

"I began to wonder, with fascination and terror, what I would do if I was indeed elected president of Chile. Then I heard the good news." The poet pointed to the posters on the truck. "Allende emerged as the one and only candidate of the Popular Unity Front. With my party's full support, I swiftly withdrew from the race. Facing an enormous and joyous crowd, I announced my withdrawal and Allende announced his candidacy."

His audience clapped louder than might be expected from the numbers in attendance, and as Neruda stepped down from the truck, eager to return to his writing desk, shells, half-written verses, and figureheads, Mario approached him and uttered two words that in themselves sounded like a request: "Don Pablo . . ."

With a subtle maneuver worthy of a bullfighter, the poet managed to avoid the boy. "Tomorrow," he said. "Tomorrow."

The postman made it through another night's insomnia by counting stars, biting his nails, sipping on a bottle of dry red wine, and scratching the skin off his cheeks.

The next morning, when the telegraph operator had the honor of viewing Mario's mortal remains, he took pity on the boy and offered him the only consolation he could think of as he handed him the bard's mail.

"You know, Beatriz is beautiful now, but in fifty years she'll be an old lady. Doesn't that make you feel better?"

But just as Mario picked up the package of letters, the rubber band holding it together loosened and allowed him a glimpse of one letter that made such an impression on him, he flew off towards the bard's house without the rest of the mail.

He found the poet enjoying a sumptuous breakfast on his terrace. Sea gulls, stunned by the sun's brilliant reflection on the sea, fluttered around his head.

"Don Pablo," Mario said sententiously, "I've brought you a letter."

The poet took a sip of his strong black coffee and shrugged his shoulders. "I'm not at all surprised, seeing as how you are my mailman."

"As your friend, neighbor, and comrade, I beg you to open it now and read it to me."

"You want me to read you one of my letters?"

"Well, you see, it's from Beatriz's mother."

He handed him the letter over the table.

"Beatriz's mother wrote to me? Mario, you let the cat out of the bag! Which reminds me of my 'Ode to the Cat.' I still think it has a few salvageable images: the cat as a salon's miniature tiger, as the secret police of the rooms in a house, and as the sultan of erotic rooftops."

"Poet, I can't deal with metaphors today. Please, open the letter."

Neruda held the butter knife up to the envelope, but he proceeded with such willful inefficiency that the otherwise simple operation took him a good deal longer than a minute. "It's true when they say that revenge is a pleasure for the gods," he thought as he lingered over the stamp on the envelope, contemplated each curl in the national hero's beard, pretended to decipher the inscrutable postmark from the San Antonio Post Office, and cautiously brushed away a crisp crumb of bread that had found its way onto the letter. The greatest detective movie could not have created more suspense, and since Mario had already chewed his nails to oblivion, he started gnawing at the tips of his fingers.

The poet began the letter in the same singsong voice he used to dramatize his poems: "Dear Don Pablo. My name is Rosa González. I am the new owner of the tavern at the bay, an admirer of your poetry, and a

Christian Democrat. Even though I would not have voted for you and I will not vote for Allende in the next election, I ask you as a mother, as a fellow Chilean, and as your neighbor here in Isla Negra, for an urgent meeting in order to discuss . . ."

At this point it was astonishment rather than a thirst for revenge that made the poet pause and read the rest of the sentence to himself. The cuticle of the postman's little finger began to bleed as an immediate consequence of the sudden gravity that spread over the poet's face. Neruda then folded the letter, glanced at the boy, and completed the recital from memory: ". . . a certain Mario Jiménez, *seducer of minors*. Thank you for your attention. Sincerely, Rosa González."

At this, he stood up, and in a tone of voice that carried deep conviction, said, "Comrade Mario Jiménez, this poet is not going to touch this can of worms even with a ten-foot pole."

Mario followed him into his room full of shells, books, and figureheads. "You can't just leave me stranded, Don Pablo. Talk to her and tell her not to be unreasonable."

"My son, I am merely a poet. I do not possess the eminent talent of disemboweling mothers-in-law."

"You have to help me because it was you who wrote: 'I do not like a house without a roof, a window without glass. I do not like a day without work, a night without sleep. I do not like man without woman or woman without man. I want lives to meet and ignite the now dormant kisses. I am the good matchmaking poet.' I guess now you'll tell me that that poem is worth as much as a bounced check!"

Two waves of emotion, one of dread, the other of stupor, seemed to sweep from the poet's liver up to his eyes. He wet his lips, suddenly so parched, and exclaimed, "According to your logic, we'd have to put Shakespeare in jail for the murder of Hamlet's father. If poor Shakespeare hadn't written that tragedy, nothing would have happened to his father."

"Please, poet, don't confuse me more than I already am. What I'm asking for is really very simple. Just talk to that woman and convince her to let me see Beatriz."

"And that would make you happy?"

"Absolutely."

"If she lets you see her daughter, will you leave me alone?"

"At least until tomorrow."

"Well, that's better than nothing. Let's give her a call."

"Right now?"

"This very instant."

As he picked up the phone, the bard could feel the boy's enormous eyes upon him.

"I can hear your heart barking like a dog. Get a grip on yourself, my man."

"I can't."

"Okay, what's the number at the tavern?"

"One."

"You must have made quite an effort to memorize it."

After Neruda had finished dialing, the postman suffered another interval of silence before the poet spoke.

"Mrs. Rosa González?"

"Speaking."

"This is Pablo Neruda." The bard had done something he usually tried to avoid: he had pronounced his own name the way a television announcer introduces the latest movie star. But the letter as well as the first sounds of the woman's voice had convinced him that he would have to pull out all the stops if he hoped to rescue his poor postman from this crisis. Nevertheless, the effect generally produced by his epic name was lost in this case and he merely received a dry "Oh" in response.

"I wanted to thank you for your lovely letter."

"You don't have to thank me for anything, sir. I just want to talk to you immediately."

"Please, go right ahead, Mrs. González."

"In person."

"Where?"

"Wherever you like."

Neruda gave himself a moment to think and then said, cautiously, "At my house, if you like."

"I'm on my way."

Before hanging up, the poet shook the receiver as if to get rid of any bits and pieces of the woman's voice that had remained inside.

"What did she say?" Mario begged.

" 'I'm on my way.' "

Neruda rubbed his hands together, and after closing

with resignation the notebook he had planned to fill
with green metaphors on his first day back at Isla Negra,
was magnanimous enough to offer the boy some sorely
needed encouragement. "At least we're playing on home
turf."

He then went over to the record player and in an
unexpectedly optimistic tone of voice said, "I brought
something very special for you from Santiago: the
postman's official anthem."

As he spoke these words, the music of "Please, Mr.
Postman" by the Beatles filled the room, upset the
figureheads, turned the sailboats around inside their
bottles, made the teeth on the African masks chatter,
loosened the tiles, split the wood, resuscitated dead
friends whose names were carved into the ceiling beams,
made the long-unused pipes smoke and the potbellied
ceramics from Quinchamalí strum their guitars, allowed
the coquettes from the Belle Époque who covered his
walls to exude their perfumes, the blue horse to gallop,
and the long, ancient train from a Whitman poem to
blow its whistle.

And when the poet placed the album cover in Mario's
arms as if submitting a newborn babe to his care and
began to dance, moving his own arms up and down like
a pelican and employing the very same steps as the
neighborhood dance champions, keeping rhythm with
those legs that had felt the thighs of exotic loves and
simple village girls and had traversed all possible roads
in the world as well as those conjured up by his
imagination, and softening the drumbeats with his

labored but tender movements, Mario was convinced that he was dreaming: these were the prolegomena of an angel, the promise of soon-to-be-achieved glory, the ritual that announced her arrival to his arms, his beloved's abundant saliva to his salty, parched lips. An angel in a flaming tunic—but with the poet's sweetness and sobriety—promised him the chimes of wedding bells. Fresh joy adorned his face and his wily smile reappeared in a form as simple as that of bread on the kitchen table. "If I die someday," he said to himself, "I want heaven to be just like this moment."

But the trains that go to Paradise are always locals that get tied up in suffocating, damp stations along the way. The only express trains are those that go to Hell. It was one such train that Mario felt he had boarded when he saw Mrs. Rosa González walking towards the house with a stride as insistent and decisive as machine-gun fire. The poet thought it best that Mario disappear behind a curtain, and then, turning around on his heels and elegantly lifting his cap, he offered his visitor the most luxurious armchair in the house. The widow refused this invitation and stood with her feet firmly planted, her legs slightly apart. Puffing out her chest, she ruled out the possibility of further digressions.

"What I have to tell you is far too serious to say sitting down."

"What is it about, ma'am?"

"For the last few months, a certain Mario Jiménez has been hanging around my tavern. This young man has been insolent to my sixteen-year-old daughter."

"What has he said to her?"

"Metaphors," the widow spit between clenched teeth.

The poet swallowed hard. "And?"

"With these metaphors, Don Pablo, he's got my daughter as hot as a pistol!"

"But we are in the middle of winter, Mrs. González."

"My poor Beatriz is eating her heart out for this postman. And he doesn't have any capital other than the fungus that grows between his toes. And if his feet are teeming with microbes, his mouth is as fresh as a head of lettuce and his tongue more tangled than a pile of seaweed. And the most serious part of it all, Don Pablo, is that the metaphors he uses to seduce her have been shamelessly copied from your books."

"No!"

"Yes! He began by innocently telling her that her smile was like a butterfly and now he's telling her that her chest is a fire burning with two flames!"

"And do you believe the image he used was visual or tactile?" the bard asked.

"Tactile," the widow responded. "I have prohibited her from leaving the house until this Mr. Jiménez clears out. You might think it cruel of me to isolate her like that, but I caught her red-handed with this poem folded up in her bra."

"Her bra was red-hot?"

The woman proceeded to unfold a piece of paper that had obviously been torn out of a school mathematics notebook and read it as if it were a judicial statement, emphasizing the word *naked* with the insight of a detective:

> Naked *you are as simple as one of your hands,*
> *smooth, terrestrial, tiny, round, transparent,*
> *you have moon-lines, apple paths.*
> Naked *you are as thin as bare wheat.*
> Naked *you are blue like a Cuban night,*
> *there are vines and stars in your hair.*
> Naked *you are enormous and yellow*
> *like summer in a gilded church.*

Crumpling up the sheet of paper with revulsion, she again buried it in her apron. "In other words, Mr. Neruda, your postman has seen my daughter in the flesh!"

At that moment, the poet regretted having subscribed to the materialist doctrine of the universe, for he felt an urgent need to beg mercy from some higher being. Instead, he risked making a plea, knowing full well that it would lack the conviction of a Charles Laughton–style lawyer who could talk a dead man back to life.

"I might venture to suggest, Mrs. González, that factual conclusions cannot necessarily be drawn from the poem."

The widow scrutinized the poet with infinite disdain. "I have known her for sixteen years, in addition to the nine months I carried her around in this belly. The poem does not lie, Don Pablo—naked, my little girl looks exactly like it says."

"My God," the poet wanted to beg, but the words remained buried in his throat.

"I am asking you," the woman continued, "his confidant and the source of his inspiration, to order this Mario Jiménez, postman and plagiarist, to refrain from setting eyes upon my daughter from this day onward, for the rest of his life. And tell him that if he does persist, I will *personally* see to it that his eyes are yanked out of his head."

Even after the widow had left, invisible particles of her being seemed to hover, vibrating, in the air. The bard said, "See you later," put on his cap, and lifted the curtain behind which the postman stood.

"Mario Jiménez," he said without even looking at him, "you are as pale as a sack of flour."

The boy followed him out onto the terrace, where the poet was trying to breathe in the fresh sea breeze.

"Don Pablo, I might be pale on the outside but I'm burning inside."

"Adjectives are not going to save you from Mrs. González's iron chains. I can just see you delivering the mail with a white cane, a black dog, and your eye sockets as empty as a beggar's piggy bank."

"But if I can't see her, what do I need my eyes for?"

"I don't care how desperate you are, in this house you are permitted to try to write poems, but not sing boleros! This Mrs. González may not carry out her threat, but if she does, you can, with total impunity, repeat the cliché that states that your life is as dark as a dungeon."

"If she does anything to me, they'll send her to jail."

"After a few hours they'll let her go. She'll claim she acted out of self-defense. She'll say you threatened her daughter's virginity with a drawn weapon, a metaphor that's as telling as a stool pigeon, as sharp as a canine tooth, and as cutting as a switchblade. Poetry's promiscuous prattle will have left its mark on your girlfriend's nipples. They hung François Villon from a tree until the blood gushed forth like roses from his neck for a lot less than that."

Mario's eyes were moist and even his voice sounded damp. "I don't care if that woman scrapes every one of my bones with a kitchen knife."

"Too bad we don't have a guitar trio here to play you a tu-ru-ru chorus."

"What hurts me is that I can't even see her," continued the postman distractedly. "Her cherry lips, her soft, mournful eyes, as if made by the night itself. Not to be able to soak up that warmth she radiates."

"From what the old lady says, it sounds more like flames than warmth."

"But why is her mother trying so hard to get rid of me? I want to marry her."

"According to Mrs. González, you don't have anything more to show for yourself than the dirt under your fingernails."

"But I'm young and healthy. I've got two lungs with more wind capacity than a bagpipe."

"But you only use them to sigh for Beatriz González. You're already starting to wheeze like the siren of a ghost ship."

"Ha! I could blow a sailboat from here to Australia with these lungs."

"My son, if you keep pining away for Miss González, a month from now you won't have enough air left in your lungs to blow out the candles on your birthday cake."

"So what am I supposed to do?" Mario shouted.

"First of all, don't shout. I'm not deaf."

"I'm sorry, Don Pablo."

Taking him by the arm, Neruda showed him the way out.

"Secondly, you should go home and take a nap. The bags under your eyes have grown deeper than a soup bowl."

"I haven't slept for a week. The fishermen call me 'the owl.' "

"And in another week they're going to put you in that wooden jacket affectionately referred to as a coffin. Mario Jiménez, this conversation is longer than a freight train. Good-bye."

They had already reached the gate and Neruda opened it ceremoniously. But as the poet was gently pushing him out onto the street, Mario suddenly froze.

"Poet and comrade," he said with conviction. "You got me into this mess and now you've got to get me out of it. You gave me your books; you taught me how to use my tongue for something other than sticking stamps on envelopes. It's your fault I fell in love."

"No way, my friend. It's one thing to give you a few of my books, and quite another to give you permission to plagiarize them. Besides, you gave her the poem I wrote for Matilde."

"Poetry belongs to those who use it, not those who write it!"

"I am overjoyed to hear you express such democratic sentiments, but let's not get so carried away that we have to vote on who the father is in a family."

As if suddenly inspired, the postman opened his bag and brought out a bottle of the poet's favorite wine. The bard could not help cracking a smile full of a tenderness that bordered on compassion. They returned to the living room, where Neruda lifted up the receiver and dialed.

"Mrs. Rosa González . . . Pablo Neruda here again."

Although Mario tried to catch her response, the words reached only the poet's poor, battered eardrums.

"I don't care if you're Jesus Christ and his twelve apostles, the postman Mario Jiménez will never set foot in this house again."

Massaging his ear, Neruda rolled his eyes.

"Don Pablo, what's the matter?"

"Nothing, my son, nothing. It's just that now I know what a boxer feels like when he's been knocked out in the first round."

On the night of September 4, word of a startling event spread rapidly around the globe: Salvador Allende had won the national elections in Chile and would become the leader of the world's first Marxist government to come to power democratically.

Mrs. González's tavern overflowed with fishermen, off-season tourists, schoolchildren with permission to play hooky the following day, and the poet Pablo Neruda, who, employing the strategy of a statesman, had preferred to abandon his refuge rather than answer the barrage of long-distance phone calls from international agencies requesting interviews. The promise of better days to come had loosened her customers' purse strings, and Rosa was obliged to release Beatriz from her imprisonment and put her to work helping with the celebration.

Meanwhile, Mario Jiménez maintained a perfectly imprudent distance. When the telegraph operator arrived in his 1940 Ford to join the festivities, the postman fell upon him and begged him to perform a small service as a go-between. Cosme finally agreed, undoubtedly because of his state of political euphoria rather than any sense of civic duty. Mario simply wanted him to wait for the right moment and then whisper in Beatriz's ear that he would be waiting for her in a nearby shed where the fishermen stored their gear.

The opportune moment arrived along with Deputy Labbé, who, dressed in white and flashing that perpetual smile, made his way through a gauntlet of taunts and boos ("Can't win 'em all!" "Win a few, lose a few!") to the table where Neruda was offering toasts, and with a princely gesture said, "Don Pablo, I guess these are the rules of democracy. We all have to know how to lose. So, the losers hereby congratulate the winners."

"Bravo, Deputy," Neruda replied as he offered him a glass of wine and raised his own. The audience clapped, the fishermen shouted "Long Live Allende" and "Long Live Neruda," and the telegraph operator walked over to Beatriz and whispered Mario's message in her ear. After taking off her apron and ridding herself of a jug of wine, the girl picked an egg off the bar and walked barefoot out into the starry night to the shed.

When she opened the door, she could just barely see the postman perched on a shoemaker's bench among the tangled nets, his face lit by the orange glow of a kerosene lantern. Mario instantly recognized that mini-skirt and tight-fitting blouse she had been wearing the first time he saw her, for it produced the same effect on him on both occasions. As if to complete his déjà vu, the girl lifted the fragile oval egg and placed it near her lips after closing the door behind her with her foot. She then slid it down her chin towards her breasts and with playful fingers balanced it on her taut stomach, eased it across her abdomen, slid it over her sex, hid it in the triangle between her legs and stared at Mario with burning eyes. He made a gesture to move, but she motioned him to be still. She passed the egg over the coppery surface of her forehead, raised it onto the bridge of her nose, and when she had brought it to her lips, placed it in her mouth and held it there between her teeth.

At that moment, Mario discovered that the erection he had sustained so faithfully for months was but an insignificant hillock compared to the mountain range now emerging from his groin, or to the not-at-all-metaphoric volcano erupting in his veins, blurring his vision and transforming even his saliva into a potentially explosive substance. Beatriz silently ordered him to kneel on the unfinished floorboards that felt to Mario like a lush, princely rug. His eyes followed the girl as she slowly drifted towards him and stood by his side.

With her own hands, she showed him how he should cup his own. If ever in the past Mario had had difficulty obeying orders, his only desire now was to be a slave. The girl leaned backwards and the egg, like a magnificent gymnast, tumbled along every last centimeter of her blouse and skirt before it dropped into Mario's outstretched palms. He looked up at Beatriz and saw her tongue flashing between her teeth, her eyes glazed but determined, her eyebrows arched, ready for the boy to take the initiative. Delicately, Mario lifted the egg as if it were about to hatch, placed it on the girl's abdomen, and with a magician's grin rolled it over her thighs and lazily traced the line of her buttocks. All the while, Beatriz's mouth was partially open and she mirrored his pulsations with her own. Once the egg completed its orbit, the boy brought it back to the arch of the belly, led it up through the cleft between her breasts, anchored it under her chin, and stood up. She gave him a smile that was more of an order than a courtesy and allowed Mario to snatch the egg with his teeth. He stepped back, and she rescued it from his lips. When he felt her lips brushing against his around the shell, he abandoned himself to the delicacies of pleasure. This first contact with her skin, which he now covered sloppily with kisses, was, in his dreams, the beginning of a surrender to a pursuit that would only end once he had explored her every pore, the most delicate fuzz on her arms, the silky wave of her eyebrows, the dizzying slope of her neck. This was harvest time: love had grown ripe, thick and hard in its bones. Words had returned to their roots. This moment, he thought, this, this moment, this, this, this, this, this moment, this, this, this moment, this. He closed his eyes as she took the egg into her mouth. In the dark, he encircled her from behind, while an explosion of sparkling fish burst forth from the otherwise calm ocean of his mind. He was bathed in the light of the incommensurable moon and felt certain, as he stroked her neck with his passionate tongue, that he knew about infinity. Again he faced his beloved and took the egg into his mouth. Now, as if both were dancing to the rhythm of a secret drummer, she held out her blouse and Mario let the egg fall between her tits. As Beatriz untied her belt and lifted up her suffocating blouse, the egg splattered on the floor. The girl pulled the blouse over her head and bared her back, golden in the light of the kerosene lantern. Mario lowered her miniskirt, and when her cunt's fragrant vegetation reached his greedy nose, his only impulse was to cover it with his tongue. At that precise instant, Beatriz let out a screech laced with heavings, sobs, extravagance, guttural cries, music, and fever that lasted entire seconds, while her body trembled until she collapsed onto the wooden floor. After placing a silent, reserved finger on those same lips that had given her such pleasure, she brought it to the rugged cloth of the boy's pants, and assessing the thickness of his member, said in a hoarse voice, "You dummy, you made me come."

...............................................................................................

The wedding took place two months after—to use the words of the telegraph operator—the floodgates had already been flung open. Aided by a mother's intuition, Rosa González was fully aware of the fact that ever since the joyous inauguration ceremony, the tournament was being played out at all times of the day and night. Mario's increased pallor could not be blamed on the common cold, an illness to which he had acquired a sudden and miraculous immunity. And Beatriz González, according to the postman's notebook (and a few casual observers), was flowering, radiant, shining, glowing, blossoming, twinkling and floating. So, when Mario Jiménez arrived at the tavern one Saturday evening to ask for the girl's hand, thoroughly convinced that his romance would be cut short and his brains and flowery tongue blown to bits by a shot from the widow's rifle,

Rosa González, a font of pragmatic philosophy, opened a bottle of demi-sec Valdivieso champagne, poured out three overflowing glasses, and accepted the postman's proposal with a phrase that bored in almost as deeply as the expected bullet: "Can't shut the stable door once the horse has bolted!"

The corollary to this piece of wisdom was uttered at the doors of the church where the already irreparable damage would at least be sanctified, soon after the telegraph operator looked at Neruda's English blue-tweed suit and exclaimed banteringly, "How elegant you look, poet!"

Neruda straightened his Italian silk tie and, with measured nonchalance, said, "This is my dress rehearsal, you see. Allende has just named me ambassador to France."

Mrs. González swept her eyes over Neruda's entire physique, from the top of his bald head to the toes of his shiny shoes, and said, "The early bird catches the worm."

As they walked down the aisle towards the altar, Neruda shared an observation with Mario. "I'm afraid, my boy, that Mrs. González has decided to confront the war of metaphors with a barrage of proverbs."

The reception was short for two reasons. A taxi was waiting at the door to take the illustrious godfather to the airport, and the young couple were just a touch impatient to find out what legitimacy might add to the activities they had carried on clandestinely for months. Mario's father, however, persuaded them to play the record "Un vals para jazmín" by Tito Fernández, a song that inspired him to give a tearful speech evoking his dead wife who was "surely watching over Mario from the heavens on this joyous day," and to carry Mrs. González onto the dance floor, where she refrained from spouting truisms while being spun around the room by this "poor but honorable man."

The postman's efforts to get Neruda to dance again to "Please, Mr. Postman" were to no avail. The poet already felt he was on official business, and so abstained from committing any act that could possibly nourish the opposition press, who after only three months were calling Allende's government a dismal failure.

The telegraph operator not only gave Mario the following week off, but also excused him from attending political meetings where the rank and file were organizing to carry out the popular government's initiatives. "You can't keep your bird in its cage and your mind on the nation," he declared with his customary metaphoric richness.

The pleasures Mario experienced in Beatriz's bed over the next few months made everything he had enjoyed until then seem like a black-and-white preview for a film now being shown in Cinerama and Technicolor. The girl's skin never disappointed him; each pore, crease, hair, even every little curl of her pubic hairs, had a new and different flavor.

One day, in the fourth month of these delicious activities, Rosa González burst into the marriage chamber, having discreetly waited outside for the girl's final orgasmic sighs, and lifting the sheets without so much as a warning, dumped the eroticized bodies they had been covering onto the floor. She spoke but one sentence, which Mario listened to in terror while trying to hide what hung between his legs.

"When I agreed to let you marry my daughter, I thought I was getting a son-in-law, not a pimp."

Young Mario watched her leave the room, slamming the door behind her. With the hope of finding comfort and solidarity, he turned towards Beatriz, a mournful expression on his face. But instead of compassion, he was treated to a grave scowl.

"My mother's right," she said, her tone for the first time alerting him to the fact that she and her mother had the same blood running in their veins.

"What do you want me to do?" he shouted, loud enough for the whole town to hear. "The poet is in Paris, so I don't have any clients to deliver the damn mail to!"

"Go look for a job!" barked his tender wife.

"I didn't get married just to hear the same shit from you I used to hear from my father!"

The door slammed again, this time so violently that the Beatles album cover fell off the wall. Mario pedaled feverishly to San Antonio, sat through a Rock Hudson and Doris Day comedy, and wasted away the next few hours watching the schoolgirls' legs in the main square and drinking beer at the local soda fountain. Next, he stopped by the post office hoping to hear some comforting words, but Cosme was busy lecturing his employees on how to win the battle of production. Two yawns later, Mario rode back to the village, but instead of returning to the tavern, he headed for his father's house.

Don José placed a bottle of wine on the table. "So, what's the matter?"

After the men had gulped down one glass, his father quickly came up with a solution.

"You've got to look for a job, my son."

Although Mario was unable to rise to an occasion of such magnitude, the mountain came to Mohammed. The Popular Unity government made its presence felt in the town when the Ministry of Tourism came up with a vacation plan for the workers in a textile factory in Santiago. A certain Comrade Rodríguez, geographer or geologist, a man with eyes as avid as his tongue, appeared one day at the tavern with a proposal for Mrs. González. Would she possibly be interested in keeping up with the changing times by transforming her bar into a restaurant and serving lunch and dinner to a contingent of twenty families that would be camping in the area during the summer? The widow was reticent for approximately five minutes; until, that is, Comrade Rodríguez informed her of the profits this new enterprise would bring in. Without hesitating, she looked compulsively at her son-in-law and said, "How would you like to take charge of the kitchen, Mario?"

In that split second, while his tender Beatriz was encouraging him with a beatific smile, Mario Jiménez felt as if he aged ten years.

"Okay," he said, gulping down his wine with the enthusiasm shown by Socrates when he drank the hemlock.

Now, in addition to all the rest of Neruda's metaphors that Mario continued cultivating and memorizing, he added a few about foods extolled by the sensual bard in his odes: onions ("round water roses"), artichokes ("dressed like warriors and sculpted like hand grenades"), eels ("enormous eels with snowy meat"), garlic ("precious marble"), tomatoes ("red entrails, fresh suns"), oils ("partridge pedestals and the heavenly key to mayonnaise"), potatoes ("flour of the night"), tuna fish ("bullets from the deep sea," "arrows in mourning"), cherries ("little cups of golden amber"), apples ("full, pure blushing cheeks of dawn"), salt ("sea crystal, the waves' lost memory"), and oranges to make *chirimoya alegre*, the dessert that would be the hit of the summer along with "Lolita at the Beach" by the Minimás.

The village was soon visited by young work crews who began installing poles from the hamlet to the highway. According to Comrade Rodríguez, the fishermen would have electricity in their homes in less than three weeks. "Allende fulfills his promises," he said, twisting the ends of his moustache. But progress brought with it certain problems. One day while Mario was preparing a Chilean salad (tomatoes, onions, and cilantro), maneuvering the knife over the tomato as if it were a dancer from a Neruda ode ("unfortunately we must murder it, sink the knife into its live flesh"), he noticed that Comrade Rodríguez's eyes had focused on

Beatriz's ass as she returned to the bar after bringing wine to his table. Only a minute later, just as she was opening her mouth to smile at a customer's request for "some of that Chilean salad," Mario leapt over the bar wielding the knife in both hands as he had seen them do in Japanese westerns, and brought it down on Rodríguez's table so vertically and with such fury that it penetrated the tablecloth and about an inch of vibrating wood. Comrade Rodríguez, who was used to geometric precision and geological surveys, did not doubt that the poet-waiter had intended this performance as a parable. If that knife penetrated a man's flesh in similar fashion, he reasoned melancholically, it would make goulash of his liver. Solemnly, he asked for the bill and decided not to enter the tavern again for an indefinite, perhaps eternal, length of time. Trained by Rosa's use of clichés—which always managed to kill at least two birds with one stone—Mario gestured to Beatriz so she would notice how fiercely the blade continued to cleave the evergreen wood even after the incident was long over.

"I get it," she said.

The profits from the new business allowed Rosa to make some investments that attracted a new clientele. The first thing she bought, on credit and with outrageous monthly payments, was a television. This brought in a heretofore unexploited group of customers: the wives of the workers in the camps, whose husbands, lulled to sleep by a sumptuous lunch conveniently washed down with heavy red wine, regularly crawled into their tents for a nap. The women consumed endless cups of mint tea, boldo tea, and broths while hungrily devouring episode after episode of the Mexican soap opera *Simply María*. During the cultural hour that followed each episode, when an enlightened Marxist militant appeared on the screen denouncing cultural imperialism and the reactionary ideas soap operas inculcated in "our people," the women turned off the TV and knitted or played dominoes.

Despite Mario's insistence that his mother-in-law was stingy—"You must have piranhas in your purse"—he had to admit that after a year of grating carrots, crying over onions, and peeling apples, he had saved enough money to turn a dream into reality: to buy an airline ticket and visit Neruda in Paris.

On a visit to the parish church, the telegraph operator spelled out his plan to the priest who had married the couple, and rummaging through the props that had last been used when the stations of the cross were dramatized in San Antonio in a production by Aníbal Reina, Sr. (more commonly known as "Rasca" Reina, a nickname his talented socialist son had inherited), they found a pair of wings decorated with geese, duck, chicken, and other assorted bird feathers that flapped angelically when activated by an attached cord. With the patience of a jeweler, the priest built a small scaffolding on the telegraph operator's back, placed a green plastic visor on his head—making him look like a gangster in a gambling house—and with Brasso cleaner shined the gold watch chain that stretched across his pot belly.

At noon, the telegraph operator walked towards the tavern, leaving behind him a trail of awestruck bathers who observed the oldest and fattest angel in all of hagiographic history crossing the burning sand. Mario, Beatriz, and Rosa, busy trying to invent a menu that would circumvent the shortage of supplies that was beginning to be felt, were all sure they were hallucinating. But when the telegraph operator shouted from a distance, "Mail from Pablo Neruda for Mario Jiménez!" raising in one hand a package with not quite as many stamps as a Chilean passport but more tape around it than decorations on a Christmas tree, and in the other hand a real live letter, the postman floated across the sand and grabbed both objects out of Cosme's hands. In a state of shock, he set them on the table and observed them as if they were precious hieroglyphics.

"Had a good wind, I see," chided the widow in a British accent, having already recovered from her oneiric vision.

"The wind was with me, but the birds were against me."

Mario held his head between his hands and shifted his eyes from one object to the other. "Which should I open first? The letter or the package?"

"The package, my son," Rosa proclaimed. "The letter contains only words."

"No, ma'am, the letter first."

"The package," the widow repeated as she made a move to grab it.

The telegraph operator raised a breeze by flapping one of his wings, and lifted an admonitory finger toward the widow's nose. "Don't be such a materialist."

The woman leaned back in her chair.

"Okay, if you think you're so smart, what's a materialist, anyway?"

"Someone who, whenever he has to chose between a rose and a chicken, always chooses the chicken," the telegraph operator replied glibly.

Mario stood up and said hoarsely, "Ladies and gentlemen, I am going to open the letter."

Since he had already decided to include the envelope, with his name spelled out in the poet's green ink, among the collection of trophies that covered his bedroom walls, he opened it with the patience and delicacy of an ant. With shaking hands, he placed the letter before him and began to read it syllable by syllable so as not to miss a single insignificant mark.

"Dear-Ma-ri-o-Ji-mé-nez-of-the-wing-ed-feet."

With one fell swoop the widow tore the letter from his grasp and began to glide over the words without pauses or intonations.

"Dear Mario Jiménez of the winged feet, fondly remembered Beatriz González de Jiménez, spark and flame of Isla Negra, most respected Rosa González, dear future heir Pablo Neftalí Jiménez González, dauphin of Isla Negra, eminent swimmer in your mother's warm uterus, and once you greet the sun, king of the cliffs, kite-and-sea-gull-chasing champion. To all four of you, greetings.

"I didn't write as soon as I had promised because I didn't want just to send you a postcard with pictures of Degas's ballet dancers. I know this is the first letter you have ever received in your life, Mario, so it had to come inside an envelope at least; if not, it wouldn't have been a real letter. It makes me laugh to think that you had to deliver this letter to yourself. I hope you will tell me everything that's going on in Isla Negra and what you are doing now that my mail comes to me in Paris. I hope they haven't fired you from the post office because the poet is gone. Or maybe President Allende has offered you a ministerial post in his government?

"Being ambassador in France is strange and uncomfortable for me. But there is a certain degree of challenge to it. In Chile, we are having a revolution *à la Chile* and we are very much admired and talked about over here. Chile's stature has grown immensely in the world . . . hmm."

"The 'hmm' is mine," the widow interjected.

"I live with Matilde in a bedroom big enough to house a warrior and his horse. But I feel very very far away from my days with blue wings in my house in Isla Negra.

"I miss you all and embrace you. Your neighbor and matchmaker, Pablo Neruda."

"Let's open the package," Rosa concluded after cutting the strings that held it together with her ominous kitchen knife. Mario picked up the letter and began looking it over carefully on both sides.

"Is that all?"

"What else do you want?"

"One of those PS things they always put at the end of letters."

"Nope, there wasn't any PS."

"It's strange that it's so short. Because if you look at it from a little ways away, like this, it seems longer."

"It's just that Mother read it so fast," Beatriz said.

"Fast or slow," Rosa replied, on the verge of destroying the string and the package, "words mean the same thing. Meaning is independent of speed."

But Beatriz missed this theorem. Her attention was, instead, absorbed by Mario's expression of utter and complete bewilderment.

"What are you thinking about?"

"That something's missing. When I learned to write letters at school, they said you always have to write PS at the end and add something you hadn't written in the body of the letter. I'm positive Don Pablo forgot something."

Rosa was digging around in the mounds of straw that filled the package until, with the tenderness of a midwife, she pulled out a Sony tape recorder with built-in microphone. "This must have cost him a pretty penny," she remarked solemnly. But when she prepared to read a note in green ink attached to the machine with a rubber band, Mario grabbed it out of her hands.

"No, ma'am. You read too fast."

He held the note out in front of him as if reading from a lectern and proceeded to recite the message in his customary syllabic style.

"Dear-Ma-ri-o-co-lon-push-the-mid-dle-but-ton."

"You took longer to read that card than I did to read the whole letter," the widow said as she feigned a yawn.

"It's just that you don't read the words—you swallow them. You have to savor words. You have to let them melt in your mouth."

He whirled a finger around in the air and brought it down upon the middle button. Neruda's voice was faithfully reproduced by Japanese technology and the poet's first word sent Mario into a frenzy: "Postscript."

"How do you stop it?" Mario shouted.

Beatriz pushed down on the red button.

"Postscript," the boy said as he danced around and planted a kiss on his mother-in-law's cheek. "I was right. PS. Postscript! I told you there couldn't be a letter without a postscript. The poet didn't forget about me. I knew that my very first letter had to have a postscript! Now I understand everything. The letter and the post-script."

"Okay," the widow answered. "The letter and the postscript. So why are you crying?"

"Who, me?"

"Yes, you."

"Beatriz?"

"Yes, you're crying."

"But how can I be crying if I'm not sad and nothing hurts?"

"You look like a professional mourner at a wake," Rosa grumbled. "Dry off your face and press the middle button once and for all."

"Okay, but from the beginning."

He rewound it, pressed the button, and there it was again, the little box with the poet inside. A sonorous and portable Neruda. The boy looked out to sea and felt as if the landscape were now complete after having been burdened by an absence for months, that now he could breathe deeply, and that the dedication "to my dear friend and comrade, Mario Jiménez" had really been sincere.

"Postscript," Neruda said again, this time louder.

"Quiet," the widow said.

"I didn't say anything."

"I wanted to send you something other than words. So I put my voice inside this cage that sings. A cage that is a bird. It is a present for you. But I also want to ask of you a favor that only you, Mario, can do. All my other friends either wouldn't know what to do or would think I was a foolish, ridiculous old man. I want you to take this tape recorder around Isla Negra with you and tape all the sounds and noises you can find. I desperately need something, even if it is only a shadow, from my home. I am not well physically. I miss the sea. I miss the birds. Send me the sounds of my house. Go into the garden and ring the bells. First tape the small bells that chime so thinly in the breeze, then pull the rope on the large bell, five or six times. Bell, my bell! There is nothing that sounds as beautiful as a bell ringing in a bell tower next to the sea. Then go down to the rocks, tape the crashing of the waves. And if you hear the gulls, tape them. And if you hear the silence of the stars, tape it. Paris is beautiful, but it is like a suit a few sizes too big for me. It is winter here as well, and the wind is like a flour mill stirring up the snow. The snow rises and rises; it crawls up my skin. I become a sad king in a white cloak. Then it rises to my mouth, covers my lips, and the words no longer come.

"And, just so you can hear some music from France, I am sending you a tape from the year 1938 that I found buried away in a second-hand record store in the Latin Quarter. How many times I sang this song when I was young! I always wanted to have it, but never could. It is called 'J'attendrai,' it's sung by Rina Ketty, and the words are: I will wait, day and night. I will wait for you to return."

A clarinet introduced the first beats, gravely and remotely, then a xylophone repeated them softly, perhaps nostalgically. And when Rina Ketty sang the verse, the bass and the drums accompanied her, the one mute and tranquil, the other whispering and lulling. Mario knew that his cheek was again wet, and even though he loved the song from the sound of the very first beat, he discreetly walked towards the beach until the surf drowned out the melody.

..............................................................................................

Mario went about the task Neruda had given him with the dedication of a philatelist.

Much to Rosa's dismay, his life and work were reduced to pursuing the waxing tide, the waning tide, and the rough waters churned up by the winds.

He tied the Sony to a rope and lowered it into crevices in the rocks where crabs sharpened their claws and the seaweed clung for dear life.

He rode out beyond the breakers in his father's boat, and wrapping his Sony in a piece of nylon, almost managed to capture in stereo the crashing of the six-foot waves that brought the driftwood tumbling onto the beach.

On calmer days, he was fortunate enough to catch the hungry snapping of the gulls' beaks just as they fell vertically upon sardines and then took off along the surface of the water, having secured their prey.

Then there was the time some pelicans—those anarchic, questioning birds—flapped their wings along the water's edge as if they anticipated the sardines that would flood in with the next day's tide, sardines the fishermen's children would collect by skimming the surface of the water with the same play buckets they used to build their sand castles. So many sardines were roasted over makeshift barbecues that even the cats feasted as they prowled under the full moon looking for their mates. Then, at around ten o'clock, Rosa saw a whole battalion of fishermen approaching her establishment, thirstier than legionnaires in the Sahara Desert.

After three hours of serving wine without the help of Mario, who was too busy taping the movement of the stars, the widow elaborated on the image of the legionnaires with a metaphor she leveled directly against Don José Jiménez: "You people came in here as dried up as a camel's turd."

While the magical Japanese machine was recording the sounds of bees at daybreak just as they reached their solar orgasms, their noses clinging passionately to the calyxes of coastal daisies; of stray dogs barking at the stars that fell into the Pacific Ocean as if it were New Year's Eve; of the bells on Neruda's terrace rung manually or capriciously orchestrated by the wind; of the foghorn from the lighthouse as it expanded and contracted, evoking the sadness of a ghost ship lost in the fog on the high seas; and of a tiny heartbeat in Beatriz González's belly first detected by Mario's eardrums, and then only with the help of the microphone—the "political and social contradictions," as Comrade Rodríguez called them while frenetically twirling the hairs on his chest, were beginning to take their toll on the harmony of this humble village.

First of all, no beef could be found to give substance to the stews. Mrs. González was forced to improvise a stock out of vegetables collected from neighboring kitchen gardens and bones so bare they didn't retain a shred of the flesh they once wore. One week after she had begun implementing this strategy on a daily basis, her customers formed a committee and a turbulent meeting ensued. They insisted—even though they were absolutely convinced that the shortages and the black market were the results of a conspiracy to topple Allende's government—that she stop trying to pass off dishwater with vegetables as real creole stew. In the last analysis, the spokesperson declared, they would accept it if it were called "minestrone"; in that case, however, Mrs. Rosa González in all decency should lower her price, even if only by a little. She did not pay the slightest heed to these seemingly reasonable arguments. Referring to the enthusiasm with which the proletariat had elected Allende, she washed her hands of the whole problem with an adage that blossomed forth from her prodigious and subtle intellect: "If you sleep with dogs, you'll wake up with fleas."

Rather than amend her ways, the widow seemed intent on following the advice given in the radical slogans of certain left-wing groups who proclaimed, with joyous irresponsibility, that one should "advance without compromise." She continued to serve brown water and call it tea, egg-flower broth and call it consommé, and minestrone and call it stew. And it was not long before other products were added to the list of impossible luxuries: oil, sugar, rice, detergents, and even the indispensable bottle of Pisco the poor tourists consumed to while away their long nights in camp.

It was onto this now carefully fertilized terrain that Deputy Labbé drove his station wagon one day to speak to the town's population. With his hair greased down like Carlos Gardel's and a smile reminiscent of General Perón's, he found a partially receptive audience among the wives of the fishermen and the tourists when he accused the government of being inept, of having halted production, and of creating the greatest shortages in the history of mankind: the poor Soviets were not as hungry during World War Two as the heroic Chilean people are today; the starving children of Ethiopia were robust coeds compared to our undernourished children. There was only one way to save Chile from the bloody and overpowering claws of Marxism: protest vociferously by banging pots and pans so that the deaf "tyrant"—as he called Allende—would paradoxically hear the people's complaints and agree to resign. Then Frei or Alessandri or any other democratic politician you might fancy could take over and freedom, democracy, meat, chicken, and color television would abound in our country.

This speech received a round of applause from some of the women and was crowned off by Comrade Rodríguez, who having precipitously abandoned his minestrone soup to hear the deputy's harangue, shouted, "You son-of-a-bitch!" Dispensing with a megaphone, trusting to his proletarian lungs, he proceeded to expand upon this compliment with some information "our little comrades" should know if they want to avoid being bamboozled by these devils wearing suits and ties who sabotage production, store food and supplies away in their private warehouses in order to create false shortages, sell themselves to the imperialists and plot with them to bring down the people's government. When the women applauded him as well, he vigorously hitched up his pants and looked defiantly at Labbé, who, trained in the analysis of objective conditions, limited his response to a wry smile and an appreciative remark about the remnants of democracy in Chile that still allowed such a high-level debate to occur in a public place.

During the following days, the "contradictions of the process," as they were called by the sociologists on television, were brought to town in a more concrete and less rhetorical form. Up until this time, the fishermen had been well provided for by a government program of extended credit as well as an extensive public relations campaign aimed at decreasing the expenditure of foreign exchange on imported meat by increasing the consumption of locally produced fish. As a result, production had continued to increase and the refrigerator truck that collected the daily catch left each day filled to capacity.

One Thursday in October, however, around noon, that vital vehicle did not appear and the fish began to wilt under the hot spring sun. The fishermen soon realized that the time had come for their poor but idyllic hamlet to suffer the same tribulations affecting the rest of the country, about which they had known, until then, thanks only to Mrs. González's television and radio. That same night, Deputy Labbé, this time in his role as a member of the truck drivers' union, appeared on television to announce a strike that would continue indefinitely, or until two simple demands were met. They wanted the president to offer truckers special prices on necessary spare parts, and, as long as he was at it, resign.

Two days later, the fish were thrown back into the sea, having infused the otherwise pleasant-smelling port with their stench and attracted the greatest number of flies and rats anyone had ever seen. Two weeks later and despite a nationwide voluntary work effort—more impressive for its patriotic fervor than its effectiveness— the country was depleted and the people pushed to the very edge. The trucks returned to the roads, unlike the smiles that remained absent from the workers' rugged faces.

..............................................................................................

Pictures of Danton, Robespierre, Charles de Gaulle, Jean-Paul Belmondo, Charles Aznavour, Brigitte Bardot, Silvie Vartan, and Adamo were mercilessly cut out of magazines and French history books by Mario Jiménez. These photos, as well as an immense poster of Paris showing the belly of an Air France jet being tickled by the tip of the Eiffel Tower (given to him by the only travel agency in San Antonio), lent the walls of his bedroom a distinctly cosmopolitan flavor. His unchecked Francophilia was, nonetheless, mitigated by a few local decorations: a banner from the Worker-Peasant Confederation of Ranquil, an effigy of the Virgin of Carmen that Beatriz defended tooth and nail against Mario's threats to exile her to the shed, a picture of Campos, the University of Chile's star soccer player from the days when the team was celebrated as the "blue ballet," a portrait of Dr. Salvador Allende decorated with the tricolor presidential sash, and one page from the Lord Cochrane Publishing House calendar commemorating the first—and until then, unending—night of love with Beatriz González.

In this pleasant decor, and after months of conscientious effort, the postman, with the help of his sensitive Sony, taped the following text, transcribed here just as Neruda heard it two weeks later in his office in Paris.

"Testing one two three. Is the arrow moving? Yeah, it's moving." (Throat-clearing.)

"Dear Don Pablo, thank you very much for the present and the letter, even though the letter all by itself would have been enough to make us all very happy. But the Sony is very good and interesting and I am using it to make up poems by saying them directly into the machine without even writing them down. Nothing great so far. It took me a while to do what you asked me because right now things are pretty tough around here in Isla Negra. They built a campsite for vacationing workers and I'm working in the kitchen of the tavern. Once a week I ride my bicycle to San Antonio to pick up the tourists' letters. Everyone is doing well and is happy and I have some really exciting news to tell you but you're going to have to wait to hear it. I bet I made you real curious, huh? Just keep listening, don't skip ahead to find it out. And since *I* can't wait to tell you the good news, I won't waste any more of your time. I just wanted to tell you that life is full of surprises, don't you think? There you are, complaining about how you're up to your ears in snow, and I have never even seen a snowflake. Except in the movies, of course. I would love to be in Paris swimming in snow, rolling myself around in it like a rat in flour. It's so weird it doesn't snow here at Christmas. I'll bet you Yankee imperialism's got something to do with it! Anyway, to show you my appreciation for your letter and your gift, I have dedicated this poem to you and also because it was inspired by your odes and it's called—I couldn't think of a shorter title—'Ode to the Snow Over Neruda in Paris.' " (Pause and throat-clearing.)

> *Soft comrade with secretive steps*
> *abundant milk from the heavens*
> *immaculate school smock*
> *the bedsheets of silent travelers*
> *who drift from hotel to hotel,*
> *a wrinkled portrait in their pockets.*
> *Light, multiple load,*
> *wings of many doves,*
> *scarf that says good-bye*

> *to who-knows-what.*
> *Please, pale beauty,*
> *fall gently upon Neruda in Paris.*
> *Dress him up in your white admiral's suit*
> *and carry him in your small boat*
> *to this port where he is so much missed.*

(Pause) "Okay, that's the poem and now here are the sounds you asked for."

"One: The wind blowing through the bell tower in Isla Negra."

(Followed by approximately one minute of wind in the bell tower of Isla Negra.)

"Two: Me ringing the large bell in the bell tower in Isla Negra."

(Followed by seven rings of the bell.)

"Three: The waves hitting the rocks in Isla Negra."

(Here follow confused sounds of waves crashing against the cliffs, probably taped during a storm.)

"Four: Song of the sea gulls."

(Two minutes of a strange stereo effect in which the person doing the recording seems to be sneaking up on some gulls, then pouncing to make them scatter, so one hears not only their screeching but also a beautifully syncopated flapping of wings. Forty-five seconds into this take, the voice of Mario Jiménez can be heard shouting, "Scat, scat, you damn sons-of-bitches . . .")

"Five: The beehive."

(Almost three minutes of dangerously close buzzing

against a background of dogs barking and unidentifiable birds singing.)

"Six: The sea retreating."

(This is a precious moment on the tape. The microphone seems to be closely following the water as it noisily retreats over the sand until each wave mingles with the next, incoming one. This could have been achieved if Jiménez had run alongside each wave, then waded into the water to capture the precise moment when the waves fused.)

"And seven" (these words are pronounced with obvious suspense, followed by a pause): "Don Pablo Neftalí Jiménez González."

(Followed by about ten minutes of a newborn's strident cries.)

.......................................................................................................

Mario Jiménez's savings, previously earmarked for an incursion into the City of Light, were rapidly consumed by Pablo Neftalí who, after sucking Beatriz's breasts dry, still demanded large bottles of chocolate milk purchased through the National Health Service, which, although sold at a discount, nevertheless depleted the family budget. One year after he was born, Pablo Neftalí not only proved himself proficient at chasing sea gulls—just as his poet-godfather had predicted—but also showed a disturbing propensity for hurting himself. He would stride up the cliffs with the sure, springy step of a cat, but his resemblance to this animal would come to an end when he reached the top. From there he would tumble down into the ocean, his behind dragging along barnacles, crabs snapping at his fingers, his nose scraping starfish, and so much water entering his orifices that his parents were sure he would die waterlogged. So, despite his firm belief in utopian socialism, Mario Jiménez got fed up with throwing potential French francs at the pediatrician, and set about constructing a wooden cage for his beloved son, thoroughly convinced this was the only way to take a nap that wouldn't end up as a funeral.

When baby Jiménez began to teethe, he took to sawing off the bars of his cage with his new molars, an activity that filled his gums with splinters and added a new claimant to Mario's rapidly declining resources: the dentist.

So, when National Television announced at noon that Pablo Neruda's acceptance speech for the Nobel Prize for Literature would be broadcast that night from Stockholm, Mario had no choice but to borrow money in order to throw the loudest, most exuberant party the region had ever witnessed.

The telegraph operator purchased a goat from a socialist butcher in San Antonio at a reasonable price—on the "grey market," as he called it. Through Cosme's good services, the party was also to be honored with the presence of Domingo Guzmán, a robust worker from the port who distracted himself from the pain of his lumbago by beating on a Yamaha drum—again, the

Japanese—at the club La Rueda to the delight of swinging hips made sensual and ferocious by the rhythms of the enormous repertory of pseudo-cumbias Luisín Landáez had introduced into Chile (with all due respect, of course).

The telegraph operator and Domingo Guzmán rode in the front seat of the 1940 Ford, the goat and the Yamaha in the back. They arrived early, loaded down with socialist buttons and little plastic Chilean flags, and presented the goat to Mrs. González, who solemnly declared that she would pay tribute to Pablo Neruda—but this wouldn't stop her from banging her pots and pans along with the rich ladies in Santiago until the communists got out of the government. "They can obviously write poetry better than they can run the country," she concluded.

With the help of the women from the reconstituted group of vacationers—this time, all devoted Allende supporters capable of knocking out anyone who dared utter a word against the Popular Unity government—Beatriz prepared a salad containing so many donations from local farmers that a bathtub had to be brought into the kitchen to bathe the tumultuous lettuce, proud celery, lively tomatoes, chard, carrots, radishes, good potatoes, stubborn cilantro, and basil. Fourteen eggs were used just to make the mayonnaise, and Pablo Neftalí was even assigned the delicate mission of spying on the hen and humming the song "Venceremos" while she laid her daily egg that would then be added to the yellow ambrosia. And, thanks to the fact that none of the women were menstruating that day, the mayonnaise was turning out nice and thick.

Mario did not miss a single fisherman's hut as he made the rounds to invite everyone to the party. He rode up and down the entire bay and through the vacationers' campsite ringing his bicycle bell and radiating the same jubilant spirit he had shown when Beatriz gave birth to Pablo Neftalí.

"A Nobel Prize for Chile, even if it is just for literature," Comrade Rodríguez was holding forth to the vacationers, "is a glory for Chile and a triumph for President Allende." He had not even finished his sentence when the young Jiménez Sr., overtaken by a sense of indignation that electrified every one of his nerves and set his hair on end, grabbed the comrade's elbow and led him over to the weeping willow tree. There, in its shade, Mario exhibited an amazing degree of self-control (gleaned in large measure from George Raft films). He let go of Comrade Rodríguez's elbow, wet his parched lips as he fumed, and said calmly, "Comrade Rodríguez, remember that kitchen knife that accidentally fell on your table one day while you were eating lunch?"

"I remember," the militant responded, massaging his pancreas.

Mario nodded, pursed his lips as if to whistle to a cat, then passed his thumbnail over his nose. "I still have it," he said.

Accompanying drummer Guzmán was Julián de los Reyes on the guitar, Pedro Alarcón on the maracas, vocalist Rosa González, and Comrade Rodríguez on the trumpet. (He thought it better to put something in his mouth, as a deterrent if nothing else.) The rehearsal took place on the porch of the tavern so everyone in town knew beforehand that they would be dancing to "La vela" (*of course*, said Radomiro Spotorno, the ophthalmologist who had made a special trip to Isla Negra to treat Pablo Neftalí's eye, the eye that the hen had cunningly pecked at the very moment the boy was examining her ass to be able to more opportunely announce the egg's arrival), "Poquita fe" for the widow, who was more in tune with that kind of corny music, and in the heavy twisting and turning category, "Tiburón, tiburón," "Cumbia de Macondo," and "Lo que pasa es que la banda está borracha" (or, It's Just That the Band Is Drunk).

Next to the television set, the postman placed a Chilean flag, the Losada editions of the poet's works opened to the page with the dedication, one of the poet's green pens, which had been procured by less than honorable means, and the Sony, which as a kind of overture or hors d'oeuvre—Mario wouldn't allow even one olive or one sip of wine to be consumed until the poet had made his appearance—played the hit parade of the sounds of Isla Negra.

Magically, at exactly 8:00 P.M., just as a delicate ocean breeze wafted into the tavern, all the commotion, clamor, practicing, and hunger ceased as National Television brought, by satellite, the concluding words of Pablo Neruda's Nobel Prize acceptance speech. For one second, one infinitesimal second, Mario felt the silence like a kiss enveloping the entire town. And when Neruda spoke through the TV's snowy picture tube, he saw the words as blue horses galloping off towards the bard's house in search of shelter in its stables.

Like children watching a puppet show, the listeners at the tavern gave the poet their undivided attention, and believed that in this way they guaranteed his real presence amongst them. The only significant change in Neruda was his suit, which replaced the poncho he always wore on his visits to the bar, the one he had on when he first succumbed to the effects of Beatriz González's beauty. If Neruda could only have watched his neighbors as they watched him, he would have seen their eyelids immobilized, as though they might miss a precious word by merely blinking. Should Japanese technology ever invent a means of fusing electronics with human beings, the people of Isla Negra could claim to have been precursors of the phenomenon. But they would do so without arrogance, full of the same humility and sweetness with which they now drank in the bard's speech.

"Exactly one hundred years ago today, a poor and splendid poet, the most profoundly despairing of all, wrote this prophecy: 'A l'aurore, armés d'une ardente patience, nous entrerons aux splendides villes.' At dawn, armed with burning patience, we shall enter the splendid cities.

"I believe in that prophecy of Rimbaud, the clairvoyant. I come from a faraway province in a country separated from all other countries in the world by its sharply defined geography. I was the most obscure poet and my poetry was regional, painful, and pluvial. But I always believed in mankind. I never lost hope. As a result, I have arrived here today with my poetry and my flag.

"To conclude, I want to say to all men of good faith, to the workers, and to the poets, that the entire future was expressed by Rimbaud in that one sentence: only with burning patience shall we conquer the splendid city that will give light, justice, and dignity to all men.

"Thus poetry will not have sung in vain."

At these words, spontaneous applause rose from the audience huddled around the set and a well of tears sprung forth from Mario Jiménez's eyes. Only half a minute into the standing ovation did he clear his snotty nose, dry off his dripping cheeks, and make his way up and down the aisles, smiling from ear to ear, thanking everyone for their warm appreciation of Neruda and offering them all his hand as if he were running for office.

The image of the poet suddenly disappeared from the screen and the telegraph operator managed to catch the next news item just as the broadcaster was saying, "We repeat: fascist commandos have bombed and completely destroyed the electrical towers in Valparaíso Province. The United Workers' Union calls on all of its members throughout the entire country to remain on alert . . ." But just twenty seconds later he was snatched from the bar by a middle-aged tourist—"ripe" is how he described her the next morning on his return from the dunes where they had gone to watch the falling stars ("falling sperm," the widow amended).

Because the truth of the matter is that the party lasted until it ended. Everyone danced to "Tiburón a la vista" three times while singing along with the chorus: "Ay, ay, ay, que te come el tiburón." Everyone, that is, except the telegraph operator, who felt gloomy from the time he heard the news report until the ripe tourist whispered into his left ear that the next song had to be "La vela."

By the time this song had been played nine times, the tourist contingent knew it so well that although it was a slow, romantic song, they accompanied it with wild shouts and hooting between sloppy kisses.

Then came a potpourri of ancient songs Domingo Guzmán had learned as a young boy that included, among others, "Piel canela," "Ay, cosita rica, mamá," "Me lo digo, Adela," "A papá le gusta el mambo," "El cha-cha-cha de los cariñosos," "Yo no lo creo a Gagarín," "Marcianita," and "Amor desesperado," sung by Mrs. González with such intensity it reminded one of the original version by Yaco Monti.

Despite the length of the night, nobody could have complained about a lack of wine. Whenever Mario spotted a table with bottles at half-mast, he filled them up *ipso facto* from a huge jug he carried around "so I don't have to make so many trips down to the cellar." There were moments during the evening when half the guests were out wandering through the dunes, and according to the widow's appraisal of the situation, the couples that sallied forth were not in all cases precisely those that had been consecrated and certified by the church or the civil registry. It was only when Mario Jiménez was certain that none of his guests could remember their names, addresses, social security numbers, or the whereabouts of their legitimate spouses that he decided the party was a smashing success and that the level of promiscuity would continue unabated without his presence or assistance. This settled, he removed Beatriz's apron with the ease of a bullfighter, grabbed her by the waist, and rubbed his member along her thigh, a gesture for which she showed her approval with sighs of delight and an abundance of tantalizing juices that lubricated her sex. His tongue wetting her ear and his hands lifting her up by the buttocks, he penetrated her right there in the kitchen without even bothering to remove her skirt.

"Someone's going to see us, my love," the girl murmured, adjusting her position to receive the full length of Mario's member.

Mario began his rotations, and as he covered her breasts with saliva he whispered, "Too bad we don't have the Sony here now to tape this homage to Don Pablo."

The very next instant, Mario had an orgasm so noisy, bubbly, wild, bizarre, barbaric, and apocalyptic that the roosters thought it was dawn and began to crow with their crests held high, the dogs confused his shrieks with the southern night siren and barked at the moon as if fulfilling an incomprehensible commitment, Comrade Rodríguez, licking the ear of a communist student, felt as if he were suddenly choking on his own tongue, and Rosa González, in an attempt to drown out Mario's Hallelujah, once again belted out the chorus to "La vela" with the microphone. Waving her arms up and down like a windmill, she urged Domingo Guzmán and Pedro Alarcón to continue banging their tamborines and drums, take out their maracas, blow trumpets, even whistle, but Mr. Guzmán stopped young Pedro with a knowing look, and said, "Take it easy, my friend. The widow's this jumpy because she knows it's her daughter's turn next."

Twelve seconds after this prophecy was uttered, when it seemed like a powerful magnet was drawing the attention of all present—drunk, sober, or unconscious—to the proceedings in the kitchen, and while Alarcón and Guzmán pretended to be wiping their sweaty palms on their undershirts before embarking on the next tune, Beatriz let loose her orgasm into the starry night with such a cadence that it inspired the couples in the dunes ("Give me one just like that, darling," the tourist said to the telegraph operator), made the widow's ears burn scarlet, and inspired the parish priest doing vigil in the tower to utter these words: "magnificat, stabat, pange lingua, dies irae, benedictus, kyrie eleison, angelica."

By the end of her last trill, the entire night seemed to grow damp and the subsequent silence contained within it something disturbed and disturbing. The widow threw her useless microphone onto the stage, and against a background of hesitant but incipient applause rising from the dunes and the cliffs, and a true cascade of appreciation from the bard's fans in the tavern enlivened by a patriotic "Long live Chile, goddammit!" from the ineffable Comrade Rodríguez, she advanced towards the kitchen, where she found her daughter's and son-in-law's ecstasy-fused eyes shining through the semidarkness. Pointing over her shoulder with her thumb, she spit these words out at the couple: "The applause is for you, lovebirds."

Beatriz covered her face, stained with tears of happiness, as a deep hot blush rose to her cheeks. "I told you!"

Mario hitched up his pants and tied them tightly with a rope.

"Okay, okay. But don't let's get embarrassed. Tonight we're celebrating!"

"And what are we celebrating, may I ask?" the widow growled.

"Don Pablo's Nobel Prize. Can't you see we won?"

"*We* won?"

Mrs. González was on the verge of making a fist, smashing it into that mischievous tongue, and positioning her toes rather bluntly against those well-nourished and irresponsible balls. Instead, arrested by a great inspiration, she decided it would be more dignified to find recourse in a proverb.

"What can't be cured must be endured," she concluded before slamming the door.

.................................................................................

According to Dr. Giorgio Solimano's records, as of August 1973, young Pablo Neftalí had suffered from the following ailments: German measles, measles, bronchitis, gastritis, tonsillitis, pharyngitis, colitis, sprained ankle, dislocated nose, contusions on the tibia, minor concussion, second-degree burns on the right arm as a result of his attempts to rescue the Spanish hen from the chicken soup, and an infected little toe on the left foot after stepping on a sea urchin so enormous it fed the entire family—with the minor addition of a touch of hot sauce, lemon, and pepper—after Mario angrily yanked it off the rock.

Mario's trips to the clinic at the San Antonio Hospital became so frequent he decided to invest the pathetic remnants of his financial backing for his now utopian trip to Paris in a small motor scooter that would make it possible for him to reach the port quickly and safely each time his son massacred a new part of his body. The vehicle also provided the family with a means of counteracting some of the effects of the more and more frequent strikes and work stoppages by truckers, taxi drivers, and grocers. Things got so bad that there were nights the tavern didn't even have bread because there simply was no flour. And with the scooter as his accomplice, Mario could shirk his kitchen duties under the pretext of scouring the town for something the widow might use to swell the contents of the pot.

"There's money. There's freedom. But there's nothing to buy!" the widow philosophized at teatime in the company of the tourists.

One night, while Mario Jiménez was reviewing Lesson Two in his book *Bonjour, Paris*, inspired by Rina Ketty's song and Beatriz, who told him that those little bubbles he made when he tried to pronounce his *R*s could, particularly on the Champs Élysées, open all kinds of doors, the deep ringing of an all too familiar bell suddenly distracted him from the irregular conjugation of the verb *être*. Beatriz watched him as he rose like a zombie, walked over to the window, opened it, and heard the full tone of the second bell, a sound that brought other neighbors out of their houses as well.

Still in a trance, he swung his leather bag over his shoulder and was about to step outside when Beatriz, stopping him with the pressure of a single finger on his shoulder, finally said something worthy of her González blood. "This town can't handle two scandals in less than one year."

She then led the postman over to the mirror, where he discovered that the only article of clothing on him, his official post office bag, barely covered one of his buns. "Tu es fou, petit!" he remarked to his own reflection.

He spent the whole night contemplating the moon as it followed its path across the sky, disappearing at daybreak. He felt such a need to speak to the poet about so many things that his unexpected return had thrown him into a tizzy. He decided that first he would ask him—noblesse oblige—about his work in Paris, why he had returned, all about the latest movie stars and this season's fashions (maybe he had even brought back a present for Beatriz), and only then would he bring up the most vital subject of all: his own complete, selected works—emphasis on the word *selected*—impeccably copied into Deputy Labbé's notebook. There was also the matter of a notice from the City of San Antonio convoking a poetry competition which offered as first prize an award, the publication of the winning text in the cultural magazine *La Quinta Rueda*, and fifty thousand escudos cash. The poet's task would be to read through the notebook, choose one of the poems, and if it wouldn't be too much of a bother, add a few finishing touches to increase his chances of winning.

Mario took up his post in front of the door long before the bakery had opened, the cowbells on the milkman's donkey had rung, the cocks had crowed, or the last streetlight had been extinguished. Sheathed in the thick knit of his mariner's sweater, he desperately searched the windows of the house for some sign of life. Every half hour he reminded himself that the bard's trip must have been exhausting, that perhaps he was lolling about under thick blankets, that Matilde was undoubtedly serving him breakfast in bed; and he never lost hope, not even when his toes started to ache from the cold, that the bard's frowning eyelids would soon appear in the window frame and he would be blessed by one of those absent smiles he had dreamt about for so many months.

At around ten o'clock, when a pale sun shone in the sky, Matilde opened the gate carrying a string bag. Joyously the boy ran up to greet her and slapped his mailbag, tracing in the air an exaggeration of what it contained. The woman held her hand out warmly, but one slight movement of her expressive eyes sufficed for Mario to perceive the sadness behind her cordiality.

"Pablo is ill."

She opened the string bag and gestured for Mario to drop the mail in. He wanted to say, "Won't you let me take it to his room?" but Matilde's soft gravity silenced him. After giving her the mail, he buried his eyes in the now empty bag, and though guessing her answer, asked, "Is it serious?"

Matilde nodded and the postman accompanied her to the bakery, bought himself a kilo of fresh rolls, and half an hour later, dropping crumbs all over the pages of his book, made the supreme decision to enter the contest with his "Pencil Sketch of Pablo Neftalí Jiménez González."

...................................................................................................

Mario Jiménez abided rigorously by the rules of the competition. In a separate envelope and not without a certain degree of embarrassment, he sent his curriculum vitae, and in order to improve the overall impression, added at the end, "numerous readings." He asked the telegraph operator to type on the address, and the ceremony was concluded by dripping wax on the seal and imprinting it with the official stamp of the Chilean Postal Service.

"Nobody can beat you for the wrapping," Cosme said as he weighed out the letter and philanthropically slapped on a few stamps gratis.

The waiting period made Mario anxious, but at least it distracted him from the daily sorrow of not being able to see the bard when he delivered the mail. Twice he managed to overhear bits and pieces of conversation between Matilde and the doctor, but he still learned nothing about the poet's health. On a third occasion, the doctor left the house and walked towards his car while Mario was hanging around outside the gate. Impulsively, Mario went up to him and asked about the bard's health. The doctor's response sent him first into confusion and later to the dictionary.

"Stable," he said.

The winning text was to be published on the central pages of a special edition of *La Quinta Rueda*, scheduled to appear on September 18, 1973, in celebration of Chilean Independence Day. One week before the anticipated date, Mario Jiménez was dreaming that "Pencil Sketch of Pablo Neftalí Jiménez González" had won and Pablo Neruda had personally handed him the award and the check, when he was rudely awakened by a series of raps on his window. Cursing, he stumbled to the window, and opening it, made out the silhouette of the telegraph operator hidden under a poncho. The next thing Mario knew, he was listening to the well-known German march "Alte Kameraden" on the tiny transistor radio Cosme had shoved into his face. Without saying a word or changing his expression, he turned the radio dial from station to station. Every one was playing the same martial music—the same drumbeats, bugles, tubas, and horns squeaking out from the radio's tiny speakers. He shrugged his shoulders and slowly, painstakingly hid the radio away under his bulky poncho, saying gravely, "I'm getting the hell out of here."

Mario ran his fingers through his wild mop of hair, grabbed his sweater, and jumped out the window and onto his scooter.

"I'm going to get the poet's mail," he said.

The telegraph operator stepped authoritatively in front of him, and pressing his hands against the handlebars, said, "Do you want to commit suicide?"

Both of them looked up at the sky and saw three helicopters flying towards the port.

"Give me the keys, boss," Mario shouted as the sputtering of his Vespa motor joined the roar of the copters.

Cosme handed them to the boy, then grabbed his fist.

"When you're done, throw them into the sea. That'll give those bastards a run for their money."

The troops had occupied all the public buildings in San Antonio and machine guns were insinuating obscenely from every balcony. The streets were almost empty, and as he approached the post office he heard gunshots coming from the north. Sporadic at first, they slowly increased in frequency. A young recruit sat smoking at the door of the post office, huddled against the cold. When he saw Mario approaching, shaking his keys, he stood up and came to attention.

"Who are you?" he asked, inhaling the last puff of smoke.

"I work here."

"What do you do?"

"I'm a postman."

"Better get on home."

"But first I have to get the mail."

"Listen, everybody and his brother is out there shooting at each other and you want to deliver the mail?"

"Hey, it's my job."

"Okay, but get the mail and then get lost."

Mario went over to the mail sorter and poked around among the letters, putting aside five for the bard. He then crossed to the telex machine, and picking up the paper that spread like a rug across the floor, found almost twenty urgent telegrams for the poet. With one quick jerk of the arm, he tore off the sheet, rolled it up, and stuffed it into his bag along with the letters. Gunfire flared up again, this time from the direction of the port. The boy surveyed the walls covered with Cosme's militant decorations. The portrait of Salvador Allende could stay put, he reasoned, because as long as the laws of Chile were not changed, he was still the constitutionally elected president, dead or alive; but Marx's bushy beard and Che Guevara's fiery eyes were torn down and buried in his bag. Before leaving, he did something that would have delighted his boss even under the circumstances: he put the official postman's cap on his head to hide the turbulent locks that now appeared subversive compared to the soldier's rigorous cut.

"Everything in order?" the recruit asked him as he left.

"Everything's in order."

"You put on your cap, huh?"

Mario touched the stiff band as if to make sure that it really was covering his hair, and with a deprecatory gesture, pulled the visor down over his eyes. "From now on, our heads should only be used to wear hats."

The soldier wet his lips with the tip of his tongue, placed a new cigarette between his front teeth, removed it to spit out a fiber of golden tobacco, and staring at his boots, said to Mario, "Go for it, man."

..............................................................................

In the area immediately surrounding Neruda's house, a group of soldiers had set up a barricade, and further away the roving lights of a military convoy flashed silently. It rained gently: a cold coastal drizzle more bothersome than wet. The postman took a shortcut to the top of a hill. Keeping close to the ground, he surveyed the situation from there: the poet's street was blocked from the north, and three recruits were watching the house from the area near the bakery. Everyone passing along this stretch of road was subject to search. In what seemed to be a relief from the tedium of patrolling an insignificant hamlet rather than an attempt to rout out subversive elements, the soldiers minutely examined every single document in people's wallets, and everyone carrying a bag was politely asked to reveal its contents one at a time: detergent, a package of needles, a box of tea, apples, a kilo of potatoes. They were then ushered on with a bored wave of the hand. In spite of the newness of the situation, the soldiers' behavior seemed to Mario somehow strangely routine. The young enlisted men stood at attention and sped up their searches only when, from time to time, a lieutenant with a moustache and a threatening, booming voice would stop by.

Mario scrutinized these activities and maneuvers until noon, when he climbed cautiously down the hill. Leaving his scooter behind, he made his way to the piers by taking an enormous detour behind the fishermen's huts. Barefoot, he slipped along under the shadow of the cliffs until he arrived at the beach in front of Neruda's house.

He stashed his bag in a cave behind a sharp-edged rock close to the dunes, and as prudently as possible, given the low, frequent flights of a helicopter scouting the shoreline, he rolled out the sheet of telegrams. For the next hour, he read them over carefully. When he was finished, he crumpled up the paper and hid it under a rock. The path leading to the bell tower was short, but very steep. His advance was continually checked by the appearance of airplanes and helicopters that had already sent the sea gulls and pelicans into exile. Their propellers allowed the helicopters to remain suspended in the air above the bard's house with such ease, they seemed like voracious beasts smelling something out. Their presence was a constant reminder that he could either fall, or be caught by the guard on the road as he tried to climb the hill. He finally realized there was safety in the shadows. It was still daylight but the cliff's overhanging edge offered him some degree of protection. It blocked out the rays of sunlight that intermittently broke through the clouds, as if to denounce even the broken bottles and polished stones lying on the beach.

Once he had reached the bell tower, he looked around in vain for a water fountain to wash the blood, sweat, and dirt off the scratches on his cheeks and hands.

He saw Matilde standing on the terrace with her arms folded, her gaze lost in the movement of the sea. She turned around when she felt the postman's presence, but he quickly brought his finger to his lips, begging her to be silent. Matilde then looked to make sure the guards on the street could not see the path to the poet's room, and with a movement of her eyes in that direction gave Mario the go-ahead.

For a brief moment, only the light from the partially closed door allowed Mario to find Neruda in the half-dark room impregnated with the smells of medicines, ointments, and damp wood. He walked across the rug towards the bed with the deference of a visitor in a temple and was shocked by the sound of the poet's arduous breathing, the way the air seemed to scrape the poet's throat.

"Don Pablo," he whispered as if adjusting the volume of his voice to the tenuous light of the lamp wrapped in a blue towel. Perhaps only his shadow had spoken. Watching the silhouettes, Mario saw Neruda raise himself with difficulty and search the darkness with dreary eyes.

"Mario?"

"Yes, Don Pablo."

The poet stretched out a flaccid arm but the gesture was lost in that game of volumeless shadows.

"Come here, my son."

When he reached the bed, Mario was stunned by the weakness with which the poet grabbed his wrist and sat him down beside his head.

"I wanted to come this morning, but I couldn't. The house is surrounded by soldiers. They're only letting the doctor through."

A weak smile appeared on the poet's lips.

"I no longer need a doctor, my son. It would be better if they just sent me straight to the gravediggers."

"Don't say things like that, poet."

"Gravedigging is an honorable profession, Mario. Don't you remember in *Hamlet* when the gravedigger says: There is no ancient gentlemen but gardeners, ditchers, and gravemakers; they hold up Adam's profession."

The boy could now see a cup on the nightstand and Neruda motioned him to bring it to his lips.

"How do you feel, Don Pablo?"

"I'm dying, but besides that, it's really nothing."

"Do you know what's going on?"

"Matilde is trying to hide everything from me, but I

have a tiny Japanese radio here under my pillow." He
inhaled sharply, then exhaled quickly and trembled.
"This fever makes me feel like a fish in a frying pan."

"It'll pass, poet."

"No, my son. The fever won't pass. It's me that will
pass."

With the edge of the sheet, the postman wiped off
the sweat that fell from the poet's forehead onto his
eyelids.

"Is it really serious, Don Pablo?"

"Well, since we were already talking about Shakespeare, I shall answer you as did Mercutio when wounded
by Tybalt's sword: No, 'tis not so deep as a well, nor so
wide as a church door; but 'tis enough, 'twill serve: ask
for me tomorrow, and you shall find me a grave man."

"Please, lie down."

"Help me get over to the window."

"I can't. Matilde let me come in here, but . . ."

"I am your matchmaker, your pimp, and your son's
godfather. With such titles earned solely by the sweat
of my pen, I demand that you help me over to the
window."

Mario tried to hold the poet back by grabbing his
wrists, but he saw the vein in his neck swell up like that
of an animal.

"There's a cold breeze, Don Pablo."

"The coldness of the breeze is relative. If you could
only feel the frozen wind that blows through my bones.
The final blow is sharp and pristine, my son. Carry me
over to the window."

"Stay where you are, poet."

"What are you trying to hide from me? What? If I open the window, won't the sea be there? Did they take that away too? Did they stick that into a cage also?"

Mario feared the poet would notice the tremble in his own voice as well as the dampness that now sprang from his eyes. He discreetly dried them and stuck his thumb in his mouth like a child.

"The sea is still there, Don Pablo."

"So what could possibly be the matter?" Neruda groaned. "Carry me over to the window."

Mario dug his hands under the bard's arms and lifted him up until they were standing side by side. He held him so tightly, for fear he might pass out, that he could feel through his own skin the path the chills took that shook the sick poet's body. Like one stumbling man, they reached the window. And as he was spreading apart the thick blue curtains, Mario did not want to look at what he could already see reflected in the poet's eyes: the red, moving light of the siren intermittently slapping his cheek.

"An ambulance," the bard laughed through a mouthful of tears. "Why didn't they just send a coffin?"

"They're going to take you to a hospital in Santiago. Matilde is getting your things ready."

"There is no sea in Santiago. Only tailors and surgeons."

The poet let his head rest against the glass, which immediately steamed up with his breath.

"You're burning, Don Pablo."

The poet lifted his eyes to the ceiling and seemed to be watching something fly off the beams inscribed with the names of his long-dead friends. A new chill alarmed the postman and alerted him to the fact that his temperature was rising. He was about to shout out for Matilde, but was stopped short by the sight of a soldier coming to give a piece of paper to the ambulance driver. Neruda made an effort to walk over to the other window but was suddenly overcome by what seemed to be an attack of asthma. While holding him up, Mario realized that the only strength left in the poet's body emanated from his head. The bard's voice and his smile were weak as he spoke, not looking at Mario.

"Tell me a nice metaphor so I can die peacefully, son."

"I can't think of any metaphors, poet, but listen carefully to what I have to tell you."

"I'm listening."

"Well, more than twenty telegrams arrived for you today. I wanted to bring them to you, but since the house was surrounded I had to leave them behind. I hope you'll forgive me for what I did, but there was no other way."

"What did you do?"

"I read all the telegrams and memorized them so I could tell them to you."

"Where are they from?"

"From everywhere. Should I start with the one from Sweden?"

"Go ahead."

Mario paused briefly and swallowed. Neruda leaned more heavily on the window ledge. A gust of wind blew against the salt-and-dust-stained panes and made them vibrate. Mario stared at a flower drooping over a clay vase and recited the first text, taking care to keep each one separate in his head.

"Pain and indignation assassination President Allende. The people and government of Sweden offer refuge to poet Pablo Neruda."

"Another," the bard said, feeling as if shadows were rising over his eyes, like waterfalls or galloping ghosts, trying to break through the glass and fuse with certain blurry bodies that could be seen rising from the sands.

"Mexico offers airplane for immediate transport of Pablo Neruda and family," Mario continued, now with the certainty that he was not being heard.

Neruda's hand was shaking as it held the window lever. Maybe he wanted to open it, but the whole time, as if he felt between his burning fingers the same thick fluid that ran through his veins and filled his mouth with saliva, he thought he saw, rising from the metallic waves that broke up the reflection of the helicopter's propellers and spread out the silvery fish into a scintillating cloud of dust, a house of rain being constructed out of water, out of a damp, intangible wood that was intimate, though only a shell. A murmuring secret was now revealed to him through his feverish blood (that black water of germination) and trembling veins (the artisanry of our dark roots); a definitive proof of the existence of an ether to which everything belongs, for which all words search, hunt, haunt with names assigned in silence (the only thing that is sure is that we breathe and then stop breathing, said the young poet from the south as he was taking his leave with a wave of a hand that had pointed to a basket of apples under a funereal bedside table): his house facing the sea and the house of water that now rose behind the panes that were also made of water, his eyes that were also the house of things, his lips that were the house of words, that let themselves be moistened mercifully by the same water that had once seeped through his father's coffin after passing through other beds and other deaths. This secret now illuminated the poet's life and death, and with that haphazard nature common to beauty and nothingness, under a deluge of dead bodies with bandaged eyes and bleeding wrists, a poem came to the poet's lips. He did not even know he was reciting it, but Mario heard it as the poet opened the window and the wind tore through the shadows:

> *I return to the sea wrapped in the sky,*
> *the silence between one wave and the next*
> *creates a dangerous suspense,*
> *life dies, the blood rests*

*until a new movement breaks*
*and the voice of infinity resounds.*

Mario hugged the poet from behind, and lifting his hands to cover his hallucinating eyes, said, "Don't die, poet."

...................................................................................................................

The ambulance carried Pablo Neruda to Santiago. Along the way, it was forced to stop at police barricades and military checkpoints.

On September 23, 1973, he died at the Santa María Clinic.

Before he took his last breath, his house at the foot of the San Cristóbal Mountain in Santiago was ransacked, the windows were broken, and everything was flooded by water running from an open faucet.

He was mourned amidst the ruins.

It was a chill spring night and the mourners drank many cups of tea until the break of dawn. At about three in the morning a young girl dressed in black defied the curfew and climbed around the hill to join the ceremony.

A pale sun shone the next day.

The funeral cortege grew as it wound its way from San Cristóbal to the cemetery. When it passed in front of the flower stands at the Mapocho Train Station, a slogan rang out to celebrate the dead poet and then another one was heard for the dead president. The troops followed alongside the march with their bayonets poised.

Near the grave, the people broke out singing "The Internationale."

...............................................................................................

Mario Jiménez heard about the poet's death on the television set at the tavern. The news was read by a pompous man who spoke about the loss of a "national and international glory." The report continued with a brief obituary note that recounted his life until he won the Nobel Prize and ended with a communiqué from the Military Junta expressing its distress at the death of the great poet.

Rosa, Beatriz, and even Pablo Neftalí understood Mario's silence and left him to himself. The dinner dishes were washed, the last tourists to ride the night bus back to Santiago took their leave, the tea bag was left brewing forever in the boiling water, and the bits and pieces of food stuck on the oilskin tablecloths were scraped at with fingernails and played with and dropped.

The postman could not sleep that night. He spent those long hours with his eyes glued to the ceiling and not a single thought distracted him. About five in the morning, he heard cars braking in front of the house. When he looked out the window, a man with a moustache motioned for him to come outside. Mario slipped his sweater on and went to the door. Another very young man with short, cropped hair, wearing a raincoat and a large necktie, stood beside the half-bald man with the moustache.

"Are you Mario Jiménez?" the first man asked.

"Yes, sir."

"Mario Jiménez the postman."

"Yes, I'm a postman, sir."

The young man wearing the raincoat pulled a gray card out of his pocket, looked it over, and blinked.

"Born February 7, 1952?"

"Yes, sir."

The young man looked at the older man and then spoke to Mario:

"Good. Come with us."

The postman wiped the palms of his hands along his thighs.

"Why, sir?"

"We just want to ask you a few questions," said the man with the moustache as he placed a cigarette between his lips and then felt around in his pockets for matches. "It's just a routine check," he remarked as he turned to his companion with a silent request for matches. The other shook his head.

"There's nothing to be afraid of," the man with the raincoat said.

"You'll be able to come right back home," said the man with the moustache, showing his cigarette to someone who poked his head through the window of one of the two cars without license plates that stood there with their motors running.

"It's just routine procedure," the young man added.

"You'll just have to answer a few questions and then you can go home," said the man with the moustache as he moved towards the man in the car, who now held a gold lighter out the window. The man with the moustache bent over, and with one flick of Deputy Labbé's finger, a strong flame shot out of the lighter. Mario watched the man with the moustache stand up. The tip of his cigarette glowed as he inhaled deeply. He gestured to the young man with the raincoat to take Mario over to the other car. The man did not touch Mario. He just pointed towards the black Fiat. Deputy Labbé's car drove away slowly and Mario walked with his escort towards the other car. A young man with dark glasses sat at the steering wheel listening to the news. As Mario got into the car, he managed to hear the announcer report that troops had occupied the Quimantú publishing house and had halted the production of various subversive magazines, including *Nosotros los Chilenos, Paloma,* and *La Quinta Rueda.*

# E P I L O G U E

**Y**ears later I read in *Hoy* magazine that one of the literary editors of *La Quinta Rueda* had returned to Chile after being exiled in Mexico. Since we were old friends from high school, I called him up and we made a date to meet. We spoke for a while about politics, especially about the possibilities of a return to democracy in Chile. I quickly grew bored with his stories of exile and, after a third cup of coffee, I asked him if, by any chance, he remembered the name of the author of the winning poem that would have been published by *La Quinta Rueda* on September 18, in the year of the Coup.

"Of course," he said. "It was an excellent poem by Jorge Teillier."

I always drink my coffee without any milk or sugar, but I have the bad habit of stirring it constantly, regardless.

"Do you remember," I asked him, "a poem that may ring a bell because of its strange title: 'Pencil Sketch of Pablo Neftalí Jiménez González'?"

My friend lifted the sugar bowl and held it in the air for a moment as he tried to remember. Then he shook his head. He couldn't remember. He held the sugar bowl near my cup but I quickly covered it with my hand.

"No, thank you," I said. "I drink it bitter."

## ABOUT THE AUTHOR

Antonio Skármeta, born in Chile in November 1940, is the author of *Chileno, The Insurrection*, and *I Dreamt the Snow Was Burning. Burning Patience* has also been made into a film, directed by the author, and a play. The film has won numerous prizes, including Best Foreign Film in France. Mr. Skármeta, who lives in Berlin, is at present a Guggenheim Fellow.

# PANTHEON MODERN WRITERS ORIGINALS

### THE VICE-CONSUL

*by Marguerite Duras, translated from the French by Eileen Ellenbogen*

The first American edition ever of the novel Marguerite Duras considers her best—a tale of passion and desperation set in India.

0-394-55898-7 cloth, $10.95   0-394-75026-8 paper, $6.95

### BURNING PATIENCE

*by Antonio Skármeta, translated from the Spanish by Katherine Silver*

A charming story about the friendship that develops between Pablo Neruda, Latin America's greatest poet, and the man who delivers his mail and stops to receive his advice about love.

0-394-55576-7 cloth, $10.95   0-394-75033-0 paper, $6.95

### DREAMING JUNGLES

*by Michel Rio, translated from the French by William Carlson*

A brilliant, hypnotic novel about an elegant French scientist who sets off to study monkeys in turn-of-the-century Africa, and about his shattering confrontation with the jungle, passion, and at last, himself.

0-394-55661-5 cloth, $10.95   0-394-75035-7 paper, $6.95

### YOU CAN'T GET LOST IN CAPETOWN

*by Zoe Wicomb*

Nine short stories powerfully evoke a young black woman's upbringing in South Africa—the ties of love and hate that bind her to her harsh land and difficult family, and that finally drive her away to exile in London.

0-394-56030-2 cloth, $10.95   0-394-75309-7 paper, $6.95

# NEW ADDITIONS TO THE
# PANTHEON MODERN WRITERS SERIES

### THE WAR: A MEMOIR

*by Marguerite Duras, translated from the French by Barbara Bray*

"At no time has [Duras's] theme of women's fidelity to memory been more movingly . . . stated than in this meditation on the horrors of World War II. . . . A complex and extraordinary book."
—Francine du Plessix Gray, *The New York Times Book Review*
0-394-75039-X paper, $6.95

### HOPSCOTCH

*by Julio Cortázar, translated from the Spanish by Gregory Rabassa*

The great Latin American writer's legendary novel of bohemian life in Paris and Buenos Aires.

"The most magnificent novel I have ever read, and one to which I return again and again."—C.D.B. Bryan, *The New York Times Book Review*

"Cortázar's masterpiece . . . the first great novel of Spanish America."
—*The* [London] *Times Literary Supplement*
0-394-75284-8 paper, $8.95

## ALSO FROM THE
## PANTHEON MODERN WRITERS SERIES

### THE SAILOR FROM GIBRALTAR
*by Marguerite Duras, translated from the French by Barbara Bray*

By the author of *The Lover*, "a haunting tale of strange and random passion." — *The New York Times Book Review*

0-394-74451-9 paper, $8.95

### THE RAVISHING OF LOL STEIN
*by Marguerite Duras, translated from the French by Richard Seaver*

"Brilliant. . . . [Duras] shoots vertical shafts down into the dark morass of human love." — *The New York Times Book Review*

"The drama proceeds savagely, erotically, and . . . the Duras language and writing shine like crystal." — Janet Flanner, *The New Yorker*

0-394-74304-0 paper, $6.95

### THE ASSAULT
*by Harry Mulisch, translated from the Dutch by Claire Nicolas White*

The story of a Nazi atrocity in Occupied Holland and its impact on life of one survivor.

"Brilliant . . . stunningly rendered." — John Updike

"A powerful and beautiful work . . . among the finest European fiction of our time." — Elizabeth Hardwick

0-394-74420-9 paper, $6.95

### THE WAR DIARIES: NOVEMBER 1939–MARCH 1940
*by Jean-Paul Sartre, translated from the French by Quintin Hoare*

Sartre's only surviving diaries: an intimate look at his life and thought at the beginning of World War II.

"An extraordinary book." — Alfred Kazin, *The Philadelphia Inquirer*

"These *War Diaries* . . . breach Sartre's intimacy for the first time."
— *The Washington Post Book World*

0-394-74422-5 paper, $10.95

### YOUNG TÖRLESS
*by Robert Musil, translated from the German*
*by Eithne Williams and Ernst Kaiser*

A classic novel by the author of *The Man Without Qualities*, about four students at an Austrian military academy and their discovery and abuse of power — physical, emotional, and sexual.

"An illumination of the dark places of the heart." — *The Washington Post*

"A chilling foreshadowing of the coming of Nazism."
— *The New York Times Book Review*

0-394-71015-0 paper, $6.95

# ALSO FROM THE
# PANTHEON MODERN WRITERS SERIES

### BLOW-UP AND OTHER STORIES
*by Julio Cortázar, translated by Paul Blackburn*

A celebrated masterpiece: fifteen eerie and brilliant short stories by the great Latin American writer.

"A splendid collection." —*The New Yorker*

"Unforgettable." —*Saturday Review*
0-394-72881-5 paper, $6.95

### THE WINNERS
*by Julio Cortázar, translated by Elaine Kerrigan*

Julio Cortázar's superb first novel about life—and death—on a South American luxury cruise.

"This formidable novel . . . introduces a dazzling writer. . . . [*The Winners*] is irresistibly readable." —*The New York Times Book Review*
0-394-72301-5 paper, $8.95

### THE OGRE
*by Michel Tournier, translated by Barbara Bray*

The story of a gentle giant's extraordinary experiences in World War II—a gripping tale of innocence, perversion, and obsession.

"The most important novel to come out of France since Proust."
—Janet Flanner

"Quite simply, a great novel." —*The New Yorker*
0-394-72407-0 paper, $8.95

### FRIDAY
*by Michel Tournier, translated by Norman Denny*

A sly, enchanting retelling of the story of Robinson Crusoe, in which Friday teaches Crusoe that there are better things in life than civilization.

"A literary pleasure not to miss." —Janet Flanner

"A fascinating, unusual novel . . . a remarkably heady French wine in the old English bottle." —*The New York Times Book Review*
0-394-72880-7 paper, $7.95

### THE WALL JUMPER
*by Peter Schneider, translated by Leigh Hafrey*

A powerful, witty novel of life in modern Berlin.

"Marvelous . . . creates, in very few words, the unreal reality of Berlin."
—Salman Rushdie, *The New York Times Book Review*

"A document of our time, in which fiction has the force of an eyewitness account." —*The* [London] *Times Literary Supplement*
0-394-72882-3 paper, $6.95

*Ask at your local bookstore for other Pantheon Modern Writers titles*